ANIMAL STORIES

Enid Blyton

Jessica

Enid Blyton titles published by Red Fox (incorporating Beaver Books):

The Adventures of Scamp

by

Enid Blyton

Illustrated by Beryl Sanders

A Red Fox Book
Published by Random House Children's Books
20 Vauxhall Bridge Road, London SW1V 2SA

A division of Random House UK Ltd

London Melbourne Sydney Auckland
Johannesburg and agencies throughout the world

The Birthday Kitten first published by Lutterworth Press 1958
The Boy Who Wanted A Dog first published by Lutterworth Press
1963
These two titles published in a Red Fox collection 1990

The Adventures of Scamp first published by Newnes 1943
Red Fox edition 1992

Red Fox edition of Animal Stories collection © 1993

The Birthday Kitten © Enid Blyton 1957
The Boy Who Wanted A Dog © Enid Blyton 1963
The Adventures of Scamp © Darrell Waters Ltd 1940

Printed and bound in Great Britain by
Cox & Wyman Ltd, Reading, Berkshire

RANDOM HOUSE UK Limited Reg. No. 954009

ISBN 0 09 922811 4

Contents

CHAPTER 1

Scamp gets his name

When Scamp was born, he had no name at all, any more than you had. He lay in a dark kennel with his mother, Flossie, the wire-haired terrier. By him were three other puppies, squeaking as they wriggled about.

In the morning Mrs Hill came to look into the kennel, and she cried out for joy. 'Oh! Flossie's got four beautiful puppies! John, come and see!'

Her husband came up and looked into the kennel. He could just see the four little puppies lying beside their proud mother.

'My, they're beauties!' he said. 'Two are black and white, and two are brown and white. Which shall we give to Kenneth and Joan?'

'Oh, we'll wait and see,' said Mrs Hill. 'They had better choose for themselves.'

Soon the two children came racing up to see the new puppies too. Their mother and father had promised them one of them for their very own, and they were excited about it. Now that the puppies were really there, they could choose the one they wanted most.

Flossie let them look at her four puppies. 'They've all got their eyes closed!' said Kenneth.

'Well, puppies and kittens always do have their eyes shut at first,' said Joan. 'Aren't they sweet? I'll pick one up and cuddle it.'

But Flossie growled when Joan tried to pick up the nearest puppy, and the little girl put it down again in a hurry. 'All right, Flossie,' she said. 'I won't hurt it. I only just want to choose one for ourselves.'

'Let's wait till their eyes are open and they can run about,' said Kenneth. 'Then we'll choose the best!'

Every day the two children went to see Flossie and the puppies. They soon grew!

'I'm sure they are growing while I look at them!' said Joan. 'And, oh, look, Kenneth – this one has got its eyes just a little bit open! It will see tomorrow!'

It was seeing already, but not very clearly. By the next day his eyes were wide open, for Flossie had licked the eyelids of the puppy with her pink tongue, and he was able to look around.

He had been able to smell before – the

nice warm exciting smell of his mother and the other puppies. He had been able to taste too, and to hear the squeals of the others, the voices of the children, the growls of his mother. Now he could see – and that was very exciting indeed!

The other three had their eyes open wide the next day. Then they began to try and waddle round the kennel. They didn't know how to use their legs at first, and they kept falling over. The children laughed when they saw them.

'Flossie, do let us take your pups on to the lawn!' they begged. 'It will be good for them to waddle about there.'

Flossie didn't mind the children having the puppies now that they were growing well. So Kenneth and Joan took them one by one on to the lawn. But the sunlight was too strong for their newly opened eyes. So they put them into the shade, and then the pups were happy.

They tried to run here and there. They fell over and got up again. They ran into the tree trunks and bumped their noses. They smelt at a hurrying beetle and wondered what it was. They tried to climb on to the children's laps, and altogether were lovely to play with.

'Well, which are you going to have?' asked Mother, as she came to watch too.

'Oh, Mother, we don't know,' said Joan. 'They are all so sweet. I love this one with the black patch on his back, and this one too with the brown tail. And this little fellow is sweet with a black patch over one eye. The other one is rather small.'

'Yes, I wouldn't have her,' said Mother.

'She isn't so well-grown as the others. And don't have the one with the black patch on one side. His head is a little too big. Choose one of the others.'

Still the children didn't know which to choose. Kenneth wanted one and Joan wanted the other. And then they both discovered that the puppy with the black patch over one eye was the naughtiest of the lot!

'Let's have *him*, shall we?' said Joan. 'I'd rather like a naughty puppy – wouldn't you, Kenneth? He'd be more exciting than a good one. Look at him, the little monkey – he's pulling the head off that flower. You scamp! Come here! Oh, stop him, Kenneth, he's just going mad in that flower-bed!'

Kenneth ran to get the puppy. It tore away from him and disappeared into the wood-shed. It tried to get under the pile of firewood there – and by the time that Kenneth reached the shed, the wood was scattered all over the floor, and the puppy was angrily chewing up the piece that had hit him on the head!

'You really are a scamp!' said Kenneth,

picking up the puppy, which at once tried to chew his sleeve. 'Look at the mess you've made with that neatly stacked firewood. Now I shall have to tidy it all up. Joan! Take this pup, and keep him quiet. He's a real scamp.'

'Kenneth! Do let's choose this one and call him Scamp!' said Joan. 'I believe he'll be the nicest puppy of the lot. Let's have him.'

'All right,' said Kenneth, with a laugh, as he watched the puppy pulling at the buttons on Joan's dress. 'Look out – he'll have those buttons off!'

Mother came up just then. 'Children!' she said, 'two of the puppies are going away to new homes this afternoon. Have you chosen yours yet?'

'Yes, Mother!' said Joan, and she held up the puppy in her arms. 'This one! He's awfully naughty.'

'Well, for goodness' sake don't choose him then,' said Mother, in alarm. 'I don't want my best hat chewed up, and all the mats nibbled!'

'Oh, Mother, we'll see he doesn't do

anything *too* naughty!' said Joan, hugging him. 'But we do want him. He's really funny – and so loving. See how he licks me!'

'Yes, he's a dear little fellow,' said Mother, 'I should think he will grow into a fine rough-haired terrier very like his mother. I like that funny black patch over his eye too. It gives him such a cheeky look.'

The puppy looked up at her and barked in a funny little high bark.

'Oh, Mother! That's the very first time he's barked!' cried Kenneth, in surprise. 'He looks rather astonished at himself, doesn't he! I don't expect he knew he could bark!'

Everybody laughed. 'Yes, we really must keep him,' said Mother. 'He's going to be an interesting little creature, fearless and faithful. He's the cleverest of the batch too. What are you going to call him?'

'Well, there's only one name for him!' said 'Kenneth. 'Scamp! Because he is a scamp, Mother.'

'All right. Scamp is a good name for a dog,' said Mother. 'Nice and short, and easy to call. Scamp! You'll soon know your name!'

Scamp almost seemed as if he knew it already. He rushed at Mother and tried to pull the laces out of her shoes. 'Don't!' she said, trying to take her feet away. 'Oh, you little mischief! Leave my feet alone!'

But as fast as she tried to take her feet away Scamp went after them, barking in his funny little high voice, his short tail wagging hard. The children shouted with laughter. In the end Kenneth had to pick him up to let Mother go back to the house in safety.

'I'm glad we've choosen you,' said Joan, tickling the puppy round the neck and under his hairy little chin. 'You're our dog now. Our very own. Did you know that?'

'And you're mine!' barked the puppy proudly. 'You belong to me! I'll look after you all my life long.'

CHAPTER 2

Scamp gets into mischief

Two of the puppies went away in a big box that afternoon to their new home. Scamp wandered about trying to find them. He had only a little sister-puppy left now, and she was the small one, and ran to shelter behind her mother if Scamp got too rough.

He liked to jump out at her and roll her over. Then he would nibble her ears and her tail, and make her squeal loudly. Flossie nipped him hard once when he was doing this, and gave him a real shock. After that he didn't tease the other puppy quite so much.

But when two disappeared to new homes he only had the little puppy left to play with, and Mother said that they must find a home for her because Scamp was so much bigger and stronger that he really was making her afraid.

So three days later the small puppy went too, and then only Scamp was left. The children were rather sad when the three puppies were gone.

'It was such fun when they were all playing around, Mother,' said Kenneth.

'A bit too much fun!' said Mother. 'Life is much more peaceful now we only have one left.'

'Well, I'm glad that one is Scamp,' said Joan. 'We are lucky to be able to keep one. Now we have a dog, a puppy, and a cat!'

Scamp knew the cat quite well. She was called Fluffy because she had a soft, fluffy coat that stood out all round her. Her eyes were as green as cucumbers, and her tail was long and wavy.

At first Scamp thought that Fluffy was pleased when she wagged her tail, but he soon found out that she wasn't!

He used to dart all around her, wuffing hard, and then her tail began to wag slowly from side to side, as she grew angry. Then, when Scamp darted at her, she wagged her tail more quickly, and began to hiss.

But the puppy, seeing her wagging tail, quite thought she was pleased and friendly, and pounced on it. Then Fluffy swung round, spat at him, and hit him hard on the nose with her paws. Once she put out her claws and scratched him so that his nose began to bleed.

Scamp was astonished. He ran crying to his mother, and she licked his hurt nose.

'You are a silly puppy,' she said. 'You must know that cats wag their tails when they are angry, not when they want to be

friends. Whenever you see a cat wagging her tail, keep right away from her.'

'Why do we wag our tails when we are pleased?' asked Scamp, settling down beside his mother. He loved her nice warm smell.

'Well, when two dogs meet one another, they are not sure at first that the other will not fight,' said Flossie. 'They cannot smile at one another, as two-legged people do, because if a dog opens its mouth and shows its teeth, it means that it is ready to bite! So dogs use their tails as signals, you see. They wag them to tell the other dog that they want to be friends, not enemies.'

'And the other dog sees and wags his tail back!' said Scamp. 'It's a good idea, isn't it! How do cats show they are friendly?'

'You will hear them purr,' said his mother. 'Now, if I were you, I'd leave Fluffy alone. You haven't claws like sharp needles, as she has – and it's no good chasing her because she can climb trees and jump on walls, and you can't. So she will only laugh at you.'

All the same, Scamp often did chase Fluffy, and it was only when the cat turned on him, flew at him, and put ten of her sharp claws into his head that he really thought it would be best not to run after her any more!

Scamp loved nibbling and chewing things. He liked to go into the nursery and see what he could find there to nibble. Sometimes he found a doll's shoe and nibbled that. Then Joan would be very cross with him and scold him.

'You bad dog! Look what you've done. You've spoilt Angela's best shoe. I'm ashamed of you.'

Then Scamp would put his tail down and look up at Joan with such sad brown eyes that she would forgive him at once. And a minute later he would be shaking the life out of Kenneth's new ball, biting big holes in it, and growling at it as if it were a wicked rat!

Once Scamp went into a visitor's bedroom. He heard somebody coming, and hid under the bed. The footsteps went by, and he began to sniff around. There was a round box under the bed. Scamp worried at it until the lid came off. There was something rather exciting in the box.

'It looks like the flowers in the garden!'

thought Scamp, as he looked at the hat inside, all trimmed with gay flowers. 'But it doesn't smell like flowers. I wonder what it is.'

He dragged the hat out on to the floor. He took it into the middle of the room and looked at it. One of the flowers shook a little and he put his paw on it. Then he began to nibble at the red roses on the hat. They didn't taste very nice. A bit of wire in one of them pricked his tongue. That made Scamp angry. He danced round the hat, barking loudly. 'What! You dare to scratch me with your claws, like Fluffy does! I'll chase you! Yes, I'll chase you. Run away and I'll come after you.'

But the hat didn't run away. It wasn't any fun at all. Scamp was cross. He pounced on the hat and the wire scratched him again. Then Scamp lost his temper and began to tear at the hat with his sharp puppy-teeth. He growled as he chewed the roses and the violets, and Auntie May, the visitor, heard him.

She came running upstairs and into her bedroom. When she saw her best Sunday hat on the floor, and Scamp chewing it hard, she gave an angry shout.

'Oh, you bad dog! Oh, you wicked dog! You've spoilt my lovely new hat! Oh, my, wait till I catch you!'

She caught up a bedroom slipper and slapped Scamp so hard with it that he yelped loudly and fled out of the room and down the stairs.

Mrs Hill heard the noise and came to see

what the matter was. When she saw what the puppy had done she was very sorry. 'I'll give you a new hat,' she said to Aunt May. 'Don't be upset any more. That puppy really is getting into too much mischief.'

Mrs Hill marched downstairs and found Scamp hiding under the table. She dragged him out and gave him a hard spanking.

'It's time you learnt what to do and what not to do,' she said sternly. The children came running in when they heard poor Scamp howling.

'Oh, Mother, what has he done?' they cried. When they heard, they looked at Scamp with stern faces. Scamp crouched down and whimpered. He felt very sorry for himself indeed.

He crept up to Kenneth and tried to lick his hand. But the boy took his hand away. Scamp was terribly upset. He went to his basket and lay down there, his head over the edge, his ears down, and his tail quite still.

He felt as if he would never be happy again – never. Even kind-hearted Joan wouldn't speak to him.

After an hour or two he crept out of his

basket and went over to Mother. She put out
a hand and patted him. He was overjoyed
and began to bark at once. His tail went up,
and he panted for joy.

'Now you are forgiven,' said Mother, 'but
you must remember not to chew things up
any more – only your own bones and balls,
Scamp. Nothing else.'

So the next time that Scamp wanted to
chew anything, he remembered his spanking and how unhappy he had been, and he
ran off before he got his teeth into it. He
was a good little fellow at learning his
lessons!

When Scamp was a little older, the
children bought him a collar. At first he
couldn't bear it. He didn't like to feel it on
his neck. He tried to wriggle it off. He put
up his paw and pulled at the collar. But it
wouldn't come off.

'What are you trying to do?' asked the dog
next door, when he met him, and saw him
trying to get his collar off by rubbing it along
the fence.

'I hate this collar-thing on my neck!' said
Scamp. 'I just hate it!'

'Well, don't you want to be properly dressed, then?' said the big dog. 'Haven't you noticed that all grown-up dogs wear collars? All men wear collars too, but little boys like Kenneth usually wear jerseys. If you've been given a collar it means that you're getting to be rather a grown-up dog. It's only puppies that don't wear collars.'

After that Scamp didn't mind his collar. He wanted to be grown-up. He felt even more gown-up than Kenneth, who still wore only jerseys. And he felt far more important than Fluffy, who wore no collar at all.

'You wait till you see what your collar's for!' said the big cat, swinging her tail. 'It's just to put a lead on when you go for a walk, so that you can't run off wherever you want to! You won't feel quite so pleased then!'

That was quite true. When Kenneth bought a lead and slipped it on to Scamp's collar, he felt cross. That horrid lead! Whenever he wanted to run ahead it dragged him back. Certainly he didn't like his collar any more.

But then Joan hung something on his collar that shone and tinkled. He wondered what it was. Flossie, his mother, told him.

'That's to say who you are, and where you live,' said Flossie. 'All dogs have to wear their name and address, you know.'

'Why?' asked Scamp, in surprise.

'Well, because their masters and mistresses love them, and don't want to lose them, of course!' said Flossie. 'If you should happen to be lost, anyone can look at the medal with your name and address on, and can bring you safely back home. Then Kenneth and Joan would be happy. Cats don't wear their names and addresses on collars. That must be because *we* are the important animals of the house, and not the cats.'

So Scamp was pleased with his collar again and showed his name and address to Fluffy.

'Pooh!' said Fluffy. 'Fancy having your name and address like that! Why, if *I* got lost, I'd know my way back without having to let people read my name and address, I can tell you! Dogs are poor creatures!'

'Woof!' said Scamp, in an angry voice. 'You're a horrid cat. I'm going to chase you.

And I'll nibble your tail *right* off this time! So look out!'

And Scamp really sounded so fierce that Fluffy thought she had better go. She ran off, her tail high up in the air, and Scamp pattered after her. Fluffy ran straight up a tree, and Scamp tried to follow. But he fell back to the ground at once and rolled over.

Fluffy sat up on a branch and laughed at him. 'You may be an important dog with your name and address on your collar!' she mewed, 'but I can climb a tree, and you can't!'

CHAPTER 3

Scamp gets into trouble

Scamp soon learnt to come whenever he was called, and to know the children's whistle at once. Wherever he was, he would come rushing to the children as soon as he heard them whistling to him.

But it was difficult to teach him not to chase anything that ran away! When Kenneth and Joan took him down to the farm lane, he saw hens wandering about all over the place. They scurried away, squawking when they saw Scamp coming, his nose to the ground!

'Ha! They're afraid of me! What fun!' wuffed Scamp to himself. 'I chase anything that runs away.'

And off he went after the hens. How they

scurried and flurried away! How they squawked and screeched! Scamp had a perfectly wonderful time.

'Scamp! Scamp! Stop it! Bad dog! Come here!' cried the children. But Scamp didn't hear a word. He had caught a hen by the leg, and was trying to get rid of a mouthful of feathers without letting go the hen.

'Oh! He's got a hen!' cried Kenneth. 'Goodness, we shall get into trouble if we don't stop him. *Scamp! Bad dog!* Come here at once.'

The wriggling hen made Scamp feel terribly excited. He still held on to it, enjoying its squawkings and clucks. The others ran away, terrified. Kenneth ran up to Scamp. He had the lead in his hand and he hit the excited dog once with it. It made Scamp jump. He let go the hen's leg at once and turned to look up at Kenneth.

'Woof!' he said. 'You hurt me! I'm sure you didn't mean to.'

'Oh yes, I did,' said Kenneth sternly. 'You were hurting that poor hen – so I had to hurt you to make you pay attention to what I was saying. Bad dog! Very bad dog! You will have to go on the lead all the way home!'

Scamp hated that. He put his tail down and went home very miserable. But all the way he kept thinking of the hens running away from him, and he longed to go down the lane again and chase them all once more! It was bad, he knew that. But perhaps if Kenneth didn't know, it wouldn't matter.

So he decided to slip off alone one morning and see if those exciting hens were still there. Off he went, his nose to the ground, smelling everything as he ran.

He soon came to the farm lane – and there, near the farmyard, were those red-brown hens wandering about loose again everywhere! What fun!

There were some tiny chicks too – little yellow and brown things, saying 'cheep-cheep-cheep!' They might be fun too, to chase, Scamp ran up to them.

Then something happened. A big fat hen ran at him, squawking at the top of her voice. How she squawked! It almost deafened Scamp. He stopped and looked at the hen. Then he made a little run at her, thinking she would turn tail and rush off like the others.

But the hen was the mother of the chicks, and she was very angry with Scamp for frightening her little ones. She was quite fearless. She didn't care how big a dog he was, or how many teeth he had – she was going to protect her little chicks!

So when Scamp ran at her, she ran at him. She put out her strong neck and pecked him hard on the nose. It made him yelp. Then she struck at him with one of her feet, and flapped round him with her big wings.

Scamp was most astonished. He got another peck that took some hair out of his ear, and he yelped. The other hens came to watch, clucking in delight.

Scamp ran back a few steps. The big hen followed, squawking loudly. She gave him a quick and spiteful peck again. 'I'll teach you to chase my chicks!' she cried. 'I'll teach you

to frighten them.' Peck – squawk – peck – squawk!

Scamp had had enough of it. He turned and fled down the farm lane, and the old hen scampered after him, screeching rude names. But she couldn't catch him up, of course. She soon went back to her chicks, and all day the other hens clucked together about the silly dog who had run away when the mother-hen had pecked him.

'That'll teach him a lesson,' they said. And

it did! Scamp never once chased a hen again. Kenneth was very pleased when he took him down the farm lane, to see the way he kept close to heel.

'I soon taught him not to chase hens,' he said to Joan. But it wasn't Kenneth who had taught him – it was the fat old hen!

Another thing Scamp had to learn was not to go into the fields where sheep are. Sheep are terrified of dogs, and soon bunch together and run off if any dog comes after them.

Two dogs were rascals at chasing the sheep. One was a big dog called Tinker, and the other was a small Scotty called Jock. Each day they slipped through the hedge into the field and made for the nearest group of sheep.

As soon as the sheep saw the dogs, they turned and ran. They frightened all the other sheep by their running, and it wasn't long before the whole flock was tearing about from side to side of the field, trying to get away from the barking dogs.

One day Scamp met Scotty, and the little dog spoke to him. 'You like a bit of fun, don't you? Well, come along with us, and you'll see some!'

'Good!' said Scamp, feeling grown-up and important. He scampered along with Scotty and Tinker, and they took him to the field where the sheep were feeding.

'Go through this hole in the hedge,' said Scotty. 'That's right. Now, you see those big grey creatures feeding over there? Well, just run after them and see how they rush away. It's such fun!'

Soon the three dogs were having a wonderful time. The sheep tore all over the place. Then suddenly a loud voice came through the air.

'I'll shoot you! You wicked dogs! I won't have dogs in my fields at lambing-time.'

'Wagging tails, it's the farmer!' barked Tinker, 'Come away, quick! He may have a gun.'

The farmer hadn't a gun that morning, or in his rage he might have shot at the dogs. As it was he managed to catch Scamp as he wriggled through the wrong hole in the hedge. He looked at his name and address.

'Oho! So you belong to the Hills, do you?'

Well, I'll just give them one warning about you – and then, you bad little dog, I'll shoot you next time you chase my sheep!'

He gave Scamp a blow that made him yell. He tore off down the lane at top speed. He felt ashamed of himself. He knew he shouldn't chase sheep. He knew he shouldn't chase hens. What would Kenneth and Joan say if they knew? But they wouldn't know, because they hadn't been there.

But they soon did know. A knock came at the door that very afternoon and outside was the farmer, looking very stern and grim.

'Good afternoon, Mam,' he said to Mrs Hill. 'I've come to give you a warning about that dog of yours. He was chasing my sheep this morning. Well, next time I see him doing that, I'll shoot him. So if you value your dog's life, you must either lock him up till the lambs are born, or you must keep him out of my fields.'

'Oh, Scamp!' said Kenneth, in dismay, when his mother told him what had happened. 'How could you be such a bad dog? You know you mustn't chase anything like that. Mother, what are we to do with him?'

'Keep him in the garden for a few days,' said Mother. 'Maybe he will forget about the sheep then. And if you always take him on a lead when you pass the sheep, he won't be able to chase them.'

Scamp was miserable. He hated being cooped up in the garden. It was such fun to wander round the country as he pleased. He felt certain he would never, never chase sheep again.

One afternoon Kenneth left the garden gate open. Scamp was out like a shot. Where should he go? He saw Scotty and Tinker on the other side of the road and he trotted over to them.

'Where are you going?' he asked.

'Down to the farm,' said Tinker, 'Coming?'

'Well, I'm not chasing sheep any more,' said Scamp. 'The farmer came to complain about me.'

'Well, you needn't chase sheep,' said Scotty. 'Just come for a walk and smell all the lovely farmyard smells, They've got some pigs down there, and we always think the pigsty smells wonderful.'

Then they passed near a field where the grey sheep were. Tinker poked his nose through the hedge. 'They look good to chase this afternoon,' he said. 'Is the farmer anywhere about?'

'I don't want to chase sheep,' said Scamp.

'Well, don't then, baby,' said Tinker, 'You're only a puppy, aren't you? We don't expect puppies to be as brave as we are!'

'I'm just as brave as any dog in the world!' cried Scamp, and he pushed his way into the field with the others. 'I'll soon show you! I'll chase more sheep than either of you!'

And he darted at three sheep nearby and yelped so loudly that they turned and fled at once. Scamp kept at their heels, enjoying the chase thoroughly.

Then suddenly there was the loud crack of a gun! *Bang!* Scamp nearly jumped out of his skin. The farmer must have come to the field! *Bang!* The gun spoke again, and Scamp turned and ran for the hedge as fast as he could. *Bang!* The gun went once more,

and this time Scamp felt somthing stinging him in half a dozen places.

'I'm shot, I'm shot!' he panted to Tinker and Scotty. 'I'm shot all over! Oh, what shall I do!'

But Tinker and Scotty weren't going to wait to look after a puppy-dog. They tore back home with their tails down, glad that they hadn't been hurt.

Scamp had many little pellets in his legs and chest from the gun. He felt tired and hurt. He began to limp. He was very sorry for himself.

'Why did I chase those sheep? I didn't really want to. I said I wouldn't. It was only because the others said I was a baby. I wish

I *had* been a baby now and not gone after the sheep. Then I wouldn't have been hurt.'

Kenneth and Joan were very upset when Scamp came limping in. Mother had to bathe his little wounds and get out the bits of shot. His fur was thick, so he hadn't really been hurt very much, but he felt as if he had.

He lay in his basket with his ears and tail down, looking very sorry for himself indeed. 'Cheer up, Scamp!' said Kenneth, patting him. 'You might have been shot dead instead of slightly hurt. But do let this be a lesson to you! Don't go chasing things any more!'

'I won't,' said Scamp. 'Except cats. All good dogs chase cats. But I'll *never, never* chase sheep again!'

And he never, never did!

CHAPTER 4

Scamp grows up

Scamp grew fast. He was a strong little dog, and very healthy. He grew well, and the children were proud of him.

'You're getting grown-up now, Scamp,' said Kenneth. 'You're a year old! Fancy that! It doesn't seem very long since you were a tiny puppy in the kennel, with eyes that were shut!'

Scamp had a deep bark now. He had lost his puppy-teeth, and had his grown-up set of strong white ones, that he bared whenever he met dogs he didn't like. Scamp was a fighter, and the children were always a little afraid that he might get hurt, for he sometimes fought dogs much bigger than himself.

'Scamp, you're such a good clever dog, and yet you won't learn that it's silly to fight!' said Kenneth. 'Why do you want to fight? There's no sense in it!'

Scamp didn't fight when he was with Kenneth or Joan. He knew they would put him on a lead if he began a fight, and he hated that. The free dogs always laughed at the dogs on a lead.

But he did fight when he was alone. He was quite a good-tempered dog really, but he simply couldn't bear it if any other dog wouldn't treat him as if he were grown-up.

One day he was very silly. He met a big dog he knew, and signalled to him with his tail to show that he was friendly. But the other dog was not in a good temper that morning. He hadn't had anything to eat, and he was hungry and cross.

So he didn't signal back to Scamp, but kept his tail quite straight and looked away.

'Why don't you greet me this morning?' said Scamp. 'Are you in a bad temper?'

'I don't always want to be seen talking to a pup like you!' said the big dog, walking off. Scamp galloped after him in a rage.

'I'm not a pup! I'm a year old! I've got my dog-teeth, not my puppy-teeth. And they're as strong as yours! I've fought heaps of dogs already.'

'Oh, go away, you make me tired,' said the big dog. 'Pups like you always boast and think there is nobody like them in the world. Go away or I'll snap one of your ears off!'

'I'll snap yours off first!' barked Scamp, in a temper, and he snapped so hard and so quickly at the big dog's ear that he managed to get a few hairs into his mouth.

The big dog turned on him at once. All the

fur rose at the back of his neck and along his back. He stared at Scamp, and lifted his upper lip so that he showed all his great strong teeth. He looked terrible.

But Scamp was not afraid, even when the big dog growled a deep growl right down in his throat. He stood quite still, and his hair, too, rose at the back of his neck. For a moment the two dogs stood there, growling fiercely – and then Scamp flung himself on the big dog, snapping hard with his teeth.

The dog tried to snap at Scamp, but the smaller dog had him by the neck and would not leave go. The big dog shook him hard and lifted him right off his legs. Then they both rolled over, growling and yelping.

And soon poor Scamp was yelping in pain because the big dog had got his teeth into him. People came running out to see what was the matter.

'Oh, that big dog is fighting the little one!' cried a woman. 'What shall we do? He'll kill him!'

A man went up to try and stop the dogs, but he was afraid of being bitten. The two angry animals worried one another, and

loud barks and growls came from them.
Then down the street came Kenneth and
Joan!

'Oh, Kenneth! Look! Poor Scamp is one
of those dogs!' cried Joan, tears coming into
her eyes. 'We must save him. We really
must.'

A man looked over a nearby wall. 'Hallo,
hallo!' he said. 'What a fight! I'd better stop
it before there's any damage done!'

'How can you stop it?' cried Kenneth. The
man gave a grin and disappeared. The
children looked over the wall. They saw that
the man had been washing his car down with
a hose. This hose he was bringing to the
wall.

'A little of this will soon bring them to
their senses!' he grinned. 'Look out!'

The hose was gushing water out strongly
from the spout at the end. The man dragged
the hose over the wall and directed the end
at the two growling dogs. A great gush of
icy-cold water fell on them. At first they
took no notice, and then, as the man went on
hosing them, they began to choke and splut-
ter. The water went into their mouths and

ears, and they had to leave go of one another in order to breathe.

The stood there, growling, soaking wet, with the drops dripping from their coats. They both shook themselves, and thousands of shining drops flew all over the place. Kenneth and Joan were soaked.

'Come here, Scamp, come here!' they

shouted. And the owner of the big dog shouted too.

'Here, Rover, here!'

The dogs took no notice of their masters, but stared at one another, their tails held quite still. They growled again. The man with the hose soaked them once more, and with a yelp the big dog turned and fled down the street. He couldn't face that icy-cold water any more! His master went after him. Scamp was left by himself, shaking water from his coat again.

Kenneth and Joan went to him. 'Poor Scamp! Your ear is bleeding. You've got a lot of fur torn out of your neck. Come home quickly and we'll bathe you. Poor old Scamp!'

Kenneth turned to the man with the hose. 'Thank you for separating the dogs,' he said. 'I should never have thought of that.'

'You're welcome!' said the man, and took his hose back over the wall. The children walked slowly home with Scamp, who looked and felt very miserable.

Soon he was lying in his basket, bathed and comforted. Mother looked at him. 'I don't feel we ought to give you too much sympathy, Scamp,' she said. 'I've a feeling that you were just as likely to start that fight as the other dog. You must learn to leave big dogs alone!'

Scamp was soon all right again. In a few days' time he met the big dog again — but to his surprise the dog signalled to him with his tail at once! He wagged it hard.

Scamp wagged his back, feeling astonished. 'That was a good scrap, wasn't it?' said the big dog. 'I shan't call you puppy-dog any more. I see you're grown-up now. It was brave of you to pounce on me. I'm so much bigger than you are. If that man hadn't separated us I might have eaten you up. Let's be friends now, shall we?'

'Oh yes!' barked Scamp, feeling proud. 'How the other dogs would envy me if I were your friend!'

'Come and walk down the street with me,' said the big dog. 'I'll show you off to my own special friends.'

He did. The other older dogs were nice to Scamp, and he wagged his tail so many times that it really felt quite tired at the end!

'He's not a puppy-dog any more,' said the big dog. 'He's grown-up, just as we are. Now, Scamp, you don't need to fight us again, to show you aren't a baby. We know you aren't. So just be sensible and good-tempered. You may grow into a bad-tempered dog if you keep fighting – and then your master won't keep you.'

After that Scamp didn't fight again, but became friends with all the dogs in the street. They didn't call him puppy-dog any more, but accepted him as one of them-selves, a grown-up dog with fine strong teeth, a deep and fearsome bark, and legs that went like the wind!

CHAPTER 5

Scamp does his best

Once Kenneth and Joan were ill. They had to stay in bed, and Scamp couldn't understand this at all.

'What's the matter with the children? Why don't they get up!' asked Scamp, when Fluffy came by. 'Are they so tired and sleepy?'

Fluffy looked at him out of her green eyes.

'They've got the measles,' she said.

Scamp didn't know what that was. He stared at Fluffy. 'Well, I've heard of *weasles*,' he said. 'They're what I sometimes chase in the fields. Are the measles cousins of the weasles? Why have the children got them? Are they keeping them for pets?'

Fluffy didn't really know what the measles

were either. She just swung her tail a little and washed her left side.

'You'd better go and ask them,' she said. 'You're such an ignorant dog. You never seem to know anything.'

'I think I'll go upstairs and see what these measles are,' thought Scamp. 'If they are anything like weasels, I might chase them round the bedroom. That would be fun.'

So he trotted upstairs and into the children's room. Mother had put Kenneth's bed in the same room as Joan's, so that they might be company for one another. They shouted in delight when they saw Scamp.

'Scamp! Why haven't you been to see us before? We've got the measles and Mother won't let us get up!' they cried.

'Woof!' said Scamp, and his nose twitched as he tried to smell where the measles were. But he couldn't seem to smell anything unusual at all. It was strange.

He poked his nose under Joan's bed. No, there wasn't a measle there. He went under Kenneth's bed. There was no measle there either! Then where could they be?

Kenneth and Joan shouted with laughter. 'Mother! Mother! I believe Scamp is looking for our measles!' cried Kenneth. 'He's hunting everywhere for something. Come out, Scamp. My measles aren't under the bed.'

Scamp came out, puzzled. He soon gave up wondering where the measles were, and put his paws up on Kenneth's bed. Kenneth patted him.

'Are you being a good dog?' he said. 'Are you guarding the house well, and barking at bad strangers?'

'Woof,' said Scamp, his head on one side as he listened to what Kenneth said.

He always did bark at strangers he didn't know and whose smell he didn't like. He knew all the tradesmen now and didn't bark at them – except the dustman. He always barked at him, and he couldn't understand why mother let the dustman take away the dustbin each week. It seemed to Scamp that the dustbin belonged to the family, and the dustman had no right to come and take it.

So he barked loudly every time the man lifted the big bin on his back – but as he always brought it back again, Scamp didn't bite him!

'And have you chewed anything you shouldn't?' said Joan, from her bed. Scamp went and put his paws up on the eiderdown there and wagged his tail.

He hadn't chewed anything he shouldn't, so he didn't put his tail or ears down as he did when he felt guilty. He had chewed his bone – and a bit of wood he had found in the garden – and Fluffy's blanket. But that was all. He felt that he had been a really good dog.

Just then Mother came in, carrying a book for each of the children.

'Little presents for ill people!' she said. 'That's the nice part of being ill, isn't it, children? People bring you things! Auntie May is coming up in a minute – and she has something for you too!'

Auntie May came up – and she brought a big bunch of black grapes. The children squealed for joy to see them.

'Oh, thank you, Auntie May! We *shall* enjoy them!'

Scamp sat and listened to all this. So the children were ill. That wasn't nice. But it *was* nice to have presents, of course. It made

them feel better. Scamp scratched
ear and thought hard.

'I love Kenneth and Joan, and I would like
to help them to feel better too,' he thought.
'I will bring them presents as well. That will
be lovely for them. I will bring them the best
presents I can think of!'

Scamp stayed with the children until their
dinnertime. They loved to hear his paws
pitter-pattering over the room, and to feel
him bump against the bed when he stood up
against it to look at them, his tail wagging as
if it were set on a spring.

Mother sent him down at dinner-time.
Then she gave the children their dinner, and
let them have some black grapes at the end.
She settled them down on their pillows and
told them to have a rest.

'Oh, but Mother, Daddy said he would
give us something nice after dinner,' said
Joan. 'Can't we wait till he comes?'

'No, he's busy now,' said Mother. 'You go
to sleep and I'll put whatever Daddy has got
for you on your beds. Then you can have it
when you wake up for tea. But go to sleep
now.'

So the children settled down and were soon fast asleep. Scamp went up to the bedroom, but they didn't say a word to him. So he pattered out again.

'I'll get them my presents,' he thought. He went into the garden and tried to remember where he had buried last week's bone. Oh, yes – under the lilac bush.

He began to scrape madly there, and then stopped to sniff. Yes – his bone was still there. He could smell it. He scraped hard again.

At last he had got the bone up. It still smelt very good. He gave it a little nibble to see if it tasted nice. Yes – the children would be sure to like that. It was his very best bone, most precious to him. He was so afraid that Fluffy or Flossie would get it that he always buried it after he had had a good nibble at it.

'Well, that's one present,' thought Scamp, and he scratched his left ear again. 'I believe I know where there are some kipper-heads. Those would do nicely for a present. I think I smelt them somewhere next door. The cat there didn't eat them.'

He squeezed through a hole in the privet hedge and went sniffing about the next door garden. Under the yew-hedge he came across two or three old kipper heads. The cat next door was very well fed and didn't always eat the kipper heads she was given twice a week.

'Ah! These are fine!' thought Scamp, taking them into his mouth. 'Wagging tails! They taste so nice that I do hope they won't slip down my throat by mistake!'

They didn't. He carried them to where he

had left his bone and then wondered if he should give the children anything else.

'I'll give Kenneth my ball, and Joan shall have the largest biscuit out of my dish,' he said to himself. 'That will please them. They are such nice children and so good to me that I'd like to give them anything I've got.'

He went to fetch his ball and the biscuit. Then one by one he took his presents to the nursery. First he took the big bone and pattered into the bedrom. The children were still asleep. Scamp put the bone gently on Kenneth's bed. Then he pattered out again and down the stairs.

He fetched the three kipper heads and put those on Joan's bed. Then he fetched the chewed ball for Kenneth and the big biscuit for Joan.

'It's a bit nibbled round the edges, but I daresay she won't mind that,' thought Scamp, as he put it on the eiderdown. Then he went downstairs again to tell Fluffy what he had done.

The children woke up about four o'clock. Kenneth stretched himself and then sniffed hard.

'What a funny smell!' he said out loud.
Joan woke up and sniffed too.

'Gracious! There *is* a funny smell!' she
said. 'It's like kippers or something.'

'Kippers! In the bedroom!' said Kenneth
scornfully. 'All the same – you're right. It's
exactly like kippers.'

'I wonder if Daddy has brought us anything whilst we've been asleep,' said Joan,
sitting up. She looked on her eiderdown and

gave a cry of surprise. 'Good gracious! Whatever's this that daddy has brought me?'

She looked at the three kipper-heads and the large biscuit. Kenneth sat up to – and saw the big dirty bone and the chewed ball. How surprised the two children were! At first they thought that Daddy had played a trick on them.

Then Kenneth gave a shout. 'Joan! It wasn't Daddy. It must have been dear, darling old Scamp! He saw other people bringing us presents because we were ill – and he thought he'd like to too!'

He's brought me three kipper heads and a nibbled biscuit!' said Joan laughing till the tears came into her eyes.

'And look at this awful old bone!' said Kenneth, holding it up for Joan to see. 'And he's given me his ball too – the one he loves so much. Joan, isn't he a generous, loving little dog?'

'He's the best dog in the world,' said Joan. 'Mother! Mother, are you there! Do come and look at the presents Scamp has brought us. Oh, Mother, it's so funny!'

Mother laughed when she came in, but

she wasn't very pleased to see the dirty bone and kipper heads on the eiderdowns. She took them off and sponged the places where they had been.

'Scamp! Scamp!' called Kenneth, when he heard the sound of pattering feet on the landing. 'Thank you, Scamp, for all the lovely presents you have brought us! We think they are the nicest we have ever had!'

'Do you really,' barked Scamp, his tail wagging fast. 'I'm so glad. They were the best I could think of. Enjoy the bone, won't you, and the kippers and the biscuit. And play with the ball as much as you like!'

Well, the bone, the kipper heads, and the biscuits disappeared, and Scamp felt certain that the children had eaten them. He didn't know that Mother had put them into the dustbin! But the ball didn't disappear – and when the chilren were better you should have seen the games they played with Scamp and his ball. He had the finest time in his life – but he deserved it for being such a generous little dog. Don't you think so?

CHAPTER 6

Scamp is a policeman

One night Scamp had an adventure. He was lying asleep in his basket when he woke up suddenly. His ears had heard a strange noise whilst he was asleep.

'Now what woke me up?' wondered Scamp. He looked at Fluffy, asleep in the basket next to his. 'Fluffy!' he said. 'Did you hear anything?'

'Only you snoring,' said Fluffy, curling herself up more tightly. 'Go to sleep and don't disturb me.'

So Scamp settled down again. But his ears stayed pricked up, and soon he heard a sound that made him sit up straight.

It seemed to come from outside, not inside. Could there be anyone outside? If so,

who was it? Nobody came at night. The tradesmen only came in the daytime and so did visitors. If anyone came at night they must be bad. They must want to steal something.

Scamp didn't bark. He got out of his basket and pattered across the floor. Fluffy woke up again.

'Have you *got* to run about all night?' she

said crossly. 'I do wish you wouldn't keep on disturbing me.'

Scamp took no notice. He was wondering how to get out into the garden and see what that noise was. The front door was shut. The back door was shut. But maybe a window was open at the bottom. He ran round the house to see.

No – not a single window was open at the bottom. Scamp ran up to the half-landing and looked at the window there. Ah – someone had left that open. He could jump out.

'But it's rather a long way to the ground,' thought Scamp, and he tried to think what was just below the window. 'Oh – it's all right, though. There's a bush below. I shall fall into that!'

He scrambled up on to the window ledge and then jumped into the darkness. He fell into the bush and lost his breath for a moment. Then he wriggled out of the bush and ran on to the grass. He stayed there, his ears up, listening.

At first he heard nothing. Then he heard a whispering sound some way off. Who could be whispering in the middle of the night?

He came to the hedge and squeezed through. Now he could hear the whispering much better. Somebody was at the back of the house. Two people. Why were they there?

'I've nearly got this window-catch undone,' he heard a voice whisper. 'We'll soon be in!'

'It must be robbers!' thought Scamp. 'Yes that must be it. Robbers! My mother has always told me to be on the look out for them at our house – and here are some next door. What shall I do? I'd better bark!'

But before he barked he ran up to the two men to smell them. They might perhaps be the people next door who had lost their key and were trying to get in at a window.

'Something touched me!' suddenly said the first man. 'I felt something touch my leg! Oooh, I don't like it.'

'Don't be silly,' whispered back the second man. 'It must have been a mouse running by.'

Then Scamp sniffed round *his* legs, and

the second man almost jumped out of his skin. 'Something touched *me* then!' he said, in a scared voice. 'I say – let's hurry up with this job and go. I'm getting jumpy.'

Then Scamp barked. Well, you should have heard him. He had a loud bark, but that night it sounded twice as loud! 'Wuff, wuff, wuff! WUFF, WUFF, WUFF!'

The men dropped their tools in a fright. 'We must run!' said one. 'Quick – that tiresome dog will wake up the whole street!'

It was a very dark night, and the men could not see. They tried to run, but one of them fell head-long over the barking dog. He fell to the ground and struck his head against the brick edge of the path. He lay still, for he had cut his head badly and had knocked himself out.

'Jim! Jim! What's up!' whispered the other man, wondering why his friend didn't get up. 'Come on. We shall be caught.'

He knelt down by Jim and tried to shake him. Then Scamp had his chance. He flew at the robber and got him by the collar. He held on for dear life, his teeth closed like a trap. He had meant to bite the man's

neck, but the robber had dodged just in time.

The robber was terrified. He did not dare to shake off the dog for fear he might fly at him again and get his teeth really into him. So he staggered about the garden in a terrible fright, trying to get over the wall at the bottom with the dog clinging to him.

But by this time the whole street was awake. Lights sprang up, and people with torches came into the gardens. They heard the tremendous growling going on in the garden next to the Hills', and they ran to see what was the matter.

'It's thieves!' cried Mr Hill, switching his torch on to the half-forced window. 'Look – here's one on the ground. He's hit his head against something and knocked himself out. The dog must have tripped him up.'

'And there's the other thief, trying to get over the wall!' cried somebody else, switching his torch on to the man and the dog.

'The dog's got him!' cried Mr Hill. 'It's Scamp! Good dog, Scamp! Hold him, hold him!'

Then a big policeman arrived, and the two men were soon taken in charge by him. The man who had been knocked out sat up and found himself surrounded by the people from the houses around.

The men were taken off. The people went back to their beds, talking excitedly. Kenneth and Joan, who had woken up, but hadn't been allowed outside, welcomed Scamp with shouts and pats.

'Oh, you good, brave, clever dog! You caught those two robbers! Oh, Scamp we *are* proud of you!

CHAPTER 7

A little quarrel

Joan wanted Kenneth to go for a walk with her. It was such a lovely afternoon.

'No, I want to do some gardening,' said Kenneth. 'My lettuces want thinning out, and I've got to cut all the dead roses off my rose trees. You go by yourself, Joan. But don't take Scamp. I do like him playing around me whilst I'm gardening.'

'Oh, but he's such good company when I'm out for a walk,' said Joan. 'He just loves a walk too. Don't be selfish, Kenneth.'

'I'm not!' said Kenneth. 'It's you that are selfish – wanting to go off for a walk when you could help me with the garden – and then wanting to take Scamp with you too, when you know how he loves being with me.'

'Well, he loves being with me too,' said Joan. 'He loves a walk much better than he loves gardening.'

Scamp came trotting up, his tail wagging. When he heard the children quarrelling, his tail went down! He didn't like that at all.

'Come here, Scamp,' said Kenneth, and Scamp went running to him to be patted.

'Good dog! I'm going to do some gardening. Coming to help me? I'll give you a biscuit if you work well!'

'Woof!' said Scamp joyfully. He loved being in the garden when Kenneth was working, because the boy talked to him all the time, and that was fun.

'Oh, Kenneth, you are mean!' said Joan, almost in tears. 'You know how I love Scamp going out with me for a walk. Well, I shan't ask him to come, because he just wouldn't know what to choose, and he'd be unhappy. I'll go by myself.'

The little girl walked off. She went down the garden path and let herself out of the gate at the bottom. It led into the lane, which was a nice place for a walk.

Scamp stared after her. So Joan was going for a walk. and she hadn't asked him to come. Kenneth was gardening, and *had* asked him to stay. But Joan was unhappy, and the dog longed to go after her to comfort her.

He looked at Kenneth, who was bending over the garden bed, whistling. Why didn't Kenneth go with Joan for a walk, then Scamp could go too, and everyone would be happy? The dog sat down and drooped his ears.

Kenneth wasn't very happy either, really. He knew it was mean of him not to let Scamp go with Joan – and Joan hadn't even tried to make Scamp go with her. That was rather nice her.

Kenneth went on working and whistling. He began to think about Joan. He wondered where she had gone – down the lane, across the field, over the little level-crossing, and along by the river. It would be nice there this afternoon.

'I hope Joan doesn't meet those rough boys we saw there the other day,' thought Kenneth suddenly. 'It's all right when Scamp and I are there, because they wouldn't dare to call names after her or chase her then – but she's alone today.'

He began to picture Joan being chased by the rough boys, and he felt more and more uncomfortable. 'I should have let her take Scamp. It was selfish of me. I didn't need Scamp – but she might. Why did I do that? It was really horrid of me. After all, I'm her brother, and I ought to see she's safe always. And she was very unselfish about it.'

Kenneth looked at Scamp. Scamp wagged his tail a little. 'I suppose you feel, too, that you should have gone with Joan?' said Kenneth. 'Well, I feel that now. I wish I'd let you go with her. If I knew which way she'd gone, I'd go after her. But I should probably go the wrong way and miss her.'

'Woof!' said Scamp eagerly. '*I* shouldn't miss her. I could smell her footsteps, you know.'

Kenneth guessed what Scamp was saying. He stood up and patted the eager little dog, who was now jumping about joyfully.

'Go and find Joan!' he said to him. 'Go and find her! Tell her I sent you, and I'm sorry I was mean. You go and find her, Scamp!'

Scamp barked loudly, licked Kenneth's hand and set off like a streak of lightning down the garden path. He pushed open the garden door with his nose and shot out in the sunny lane. Fluffy was on the wall there, just by the door, and she stared at him in surprise.

'What's up with you?' she asked. 'Can you smell the butcher boy coming, or something?'

'No,' said Scamp, his nose to the ground. 'I am going to find Joan.'

'Oh,' said Fluffy, 'well, she went down the lane. I saw her.'

'You needn't tell *me* that !' barked Scamp. 'My nose has already told me! I can smell her footsteps – here they go – down this

side of the lane – and into the ditch to pick a flower – and over to the other side to see something else – and then down the middle of the lane. Here I go! I'll soon find Joan!'

CHAPTER 8

Scamp is a hero

Joan wasn't enjoying her walk very much. She felt cross with Kenneth, and she missed Scamp. It was such fun when he came for walks – he always danced round them, ran after sticks they threw, rolled over and over in the grass, and altogether went quite mad. It was lonely without him.

The river was lovely that afternoon. It flowed along, smooth and blue and glittering.

The little girl ran along by the water. She suddenly saw a moorhen swimming along near the bank, its little black head bobbing to and fro as if it went by clockwork. She laughed. 'You're sweet!' she said. 'Have you any babies? I wish I could see them. Moorhen chicks are lovely!'

The moorhen had some chicks. They were swimming after her in a long line, very small indeed. When the moorhen saw Joan she was frightened. She called to her chicks at once.

'Look out! That girl might be an enemy and throw stones. Our old nest is quite near here. Follow me and we will hide in it till she is gone.'

She swam to where the old nest, made of flattened rushes, lay hidden in a tiny cove nearby. The chicks scrambled up into it, and squatted down, quite quiet.

Joan wondered where they had gone. She went to see. She caught sight of the nest, and exclaimed in delight.

'Oh! You're all in your old nest! Oh, I really must get nearer and see you!'

She put a foot carefully on to a clump of rushes. Then her left foot went on to another clump of rushes. The little girl bend over to see the moorhen's nest and chicks.

Her foot suddenly slipped. She flung out her hands to try and get her balance, but she

couldn't, for the rushes were so slippery to
tread on. She fell headlong into the water
with such a splash that all the chicks were
terrified and slipped out of their nest to hide
under the water.

Joan struck out with her hands to try and
get to the bank. She couldn't swim, but she
thought she could soon get to the bank. The
water was very deep there. She pulled hard
at some rushes, but instead of helping her,

they gave way, and she fell back into deeper water.

Then the current of the river caught her and began to move her away from the bank. She screamed. 'Help! Help! Oh, help me, someone! I'm in the water!'

And where was Scamp He had just gone over the little level-crossing, and was running to the riverside. He stood there and looked. There was no sign of Joan anywhere. She must have gone a very long way!

The dog put his nose to the ground and went along by the water, sniffing where the little girl had walked. Then suddenly a faint, far-off sound came to his ears. Why, it was Joan's voice. She must be in trouble! But where could she be? There wasn't a sign of her anywhere.

Scamp looked into the water – and there, swung out to the middle of the river by the strong current, was poor Joan still struggling hard.

'I'm coming!' barked Scamp loudly. And into the water he leapt at once. He swam strongly towards the little girl, his nose just above the surface. He could not swim very fast, but he did the best he could.

His heart was beating fast, and he was panting when he reached the little girl. He caught hold of her dress, and turned himself round towards the bank. Somehow he must get her there before she sank under the water and disappeared!

It was hard work, for Joan was heavy and her clothes were full of water. But the dog

would not give up. He worked his legs steadily, though he felt as if he really could not possibly swim even halfway to the bank with such a heavy load to drag. But it was Joan – the little girl he loved! He had to save her, even if his beating heart burst itself.

When they got near the bank Joan managed to clutch some strong tufts of rushes and pulled herself in. She lay on the sloping bank wet and frightened – but safe! Scamp shook himself, and then went to lick Joan. He was frightened too, and worried – but so glad that he had been able to save Joan when she was in danger. What a good thing Kenneth had let him go after her!

When Joan felt better, she stood up rather unsteadily, and began to walk slowly home. Scamp ran beside her. They met no one, and at last Joan went through the garden door and into the back garden of her home. Kenneth was still there gardening.

Joan sank down on the grass beside him and told him in a faint voice all that had happened. 'And if it hadn't been for dear old darling Scamp, I'd have been drowned,' she said. 'I'm sure I would. Oh, Kenneth, he was wonderful. He's a real hero! Dear old Scamp!'

Kenneth put his arms round Joan and lifted her up. 'It's all my fault!' he said. 'I should have come with you. Come indoors. You're shivering. You must change your clothes. Poor Joan.'

Joan was soon out of her wet clothes and into a warm bed. Mother fussed over her, and Joan began to feel she had had quite an adventure. When Daddy came home he had to hear all about it too, and he looked rather grave.

'You mustn't walk alone by the river again,' he told Joan. 'You must always take Scamp. Good dog! What should we do without you? You're a hero, Scamp! Did you know that? Yes – a real hero!'

Scamp didn't know what a hero was, but he thought it must be something nice as Mr Hill said it in such a proud voice. He wagged his tail hard, and ran off to find Fluffy.

'Hallo,' he said. 'Did you know I was a hero? The master just said I was.'

'Well, he's made a mistake,' said Fluffy,

washing her face. 'You're no hero! You're just a tiresome little dog with much too loud a bark!'

And that was all that Scamp got out of Fluffy! But the others made up for it – they gave him a fine new rubber ball, and emptied a tin of his favourite sardines into his dish, and bought him the biggest and juiciest bone he had ever had.

'You're better than a hero!' said Joan,

hugging him. 'Scamp, you're the dearest and the best dog that ever lived. How do you like that?'

Well – Scamp liked it very much indeed. I think Joan was right, don't you!

The Birthday Kitten

by

Enid Blyton

Illustrated by Joyce Smith

RED FOX

CONTENTS

1.   *"WHAT DO YOU WANT FOR YOUR BIRTHDAY?"*

"TWINS! You'd better begin to think what you want for your birthday!" said Mummy. "Granny was asking me what you'd like yesterday—and Auntie Sue asked me today."

"Oh! Yes, we'll think of our list straight away!" said Terry. "Come on, Tessie. I've got my pencil. Now—we want some new snap-cards, don't we? Ours are so dirty!"

"Yes. And I'd love a new pencil-box," said Tessie. "Someone dropped mine at school the other day, and the lid broke."

Terry wrote "Tessie" at the top of one side of his piece of paper, and "Terry" on the other. "Now," he said, "that's PENCIL-BOX for you, Tessie—and I'll put SNAP-CARDS down for me. And I want a book too—about animals." He wrote that down under his own name.

"I'd like a book about birds," said Tessie. "And I know the one I want. I saw it in a book-shop the other day. I'll write down the title for you."

"It would be a good idea to put BOOK-

TOKENS too," said Terry, nibbling the end of his pencil. "Mummy, can we put BOOK-TOKENS? Sometimes Granpa gives us such a dull book, and it's a waste of reading then. But if he gave us a book-token it means we can go round the book-shop by ourselves and choose what we really like."

"Of course put that down," said Mummy. "You always choose sensible books. But put a few other things besides those you've already written, Terry. You won't get everything you want, but at least there will be plenty for people to choose from."

"Well, let's put down a new doll for you, Tessie, and a new clockwork car for me," said Terry. "And what about a jigsaw or some other game? And I'd love some paints."

The lists grew quite long. Terry whispered to Tessie and she nodded.

"What are you whispering about?" asked Mummy, smiling. "Something special?"

"Yes," said Terry. "I was wondering if it's any use putting down what we *always* put down and never get, Mummy."

"What's that?" asked his mother.

"Well—we *always* put down a puppy or a

kitten," said Terry. "Always. But we've never had one yet."

"Last Christmas I put down PUPPY three times on my list," said Tessie, "and I got one— but it was a *toy* one! Just a nightdress case that

"I don't really want any animals"

holds my nightie beautifully—but I want a *live* one. Or a kitten—I don't mind which!"

"*Is* it any good putting down puppy or kitten again, Mummy?" said Terry.

"Well—I don't really want any animals till Baby is bigger," said Mummy. "And then, you know, they cost money to feed if you are going to keep them properly—and a dog needs a kennel, because I couldn't have him in the house while Baby is so small."

"I don't see *why*," began Tessie. "*We* could look after him. I'd love to."

"Darling, you are at school all day, except in the week-ends and holidays," said her mother. "Wait till Baby is bigger."

"We've waited so long," said Terry mournfully. "We're almost nine—and except for a hedgehog I kept out in the garden shed one winter, and a robin with a broken leg we kept till it mended, we've never had a proper pet."

"I suppose, then, Mummy, it *isn't* any good putting down a puppy or kitten on our list?" said Tessie.

"Not while Baby is small," said her mother. "I don't want to trip over animals when I'm carrying Baby about. What about putting down a canary? You could have that, if you like to look after it properly each day."

"Yes. That's a good idea. We'll put down canary," said Terry, and wrote it down under both their names in big letters "CANARY". "It doesn't matter which of us has it, we can share it. I only hope we get a cage with it!"

It seemed a long time before their birthday came. They always shared one between them because they were twins. Their mother made them a marvellous cake. She was icing it in the kitchen when they came running in from school one afternoon.

"Oh, go out of the kitchen, quickly!" said Mummy. "You mustn't see your cake yet! Terry, look in the dining-room cupboard for me, please, and see if you can find a packet of tiny birthday-cake candles. Count out eighteen—nine for each of you—and bring them to me."

"Birthdays *are* exciting!" said Tessie as she went with Terry to the dining-room. "Terry—do you think we're going to have a puppy or kitten—or perhaps a canary?"

"I don't know," said Terry, hunting in the cupboard. "I haven't heard a whine or a bark or a mew or a trill at all, not *anywhere* in the house. Have you?"

"No. I haven't," said Tessie. "Isn't it a pity we're so very fond of animals and haven't any—and Bill over the road has a dog and rabbits and mice—and really doesn't like them much. He's always forgetting to feed them. It doesn't seem fair."

"Lots of things aren't fair," said Terry. "But you just can't do anything about it! Here are the candles at last—in this corner. I'll count out eighteen into your hand, Tessie. Fancy—eighteen —isn't it a lot! I'm glad we're twins and have a double birthday."

They took the candles back to Mother—and just as they were going out of the kitchen, they heard a funny squeak! They stopped at once and looked at one another.

"A puppy!" whispered Terry. "I'm sure it was! Listen!"

They stood in the hall and listened again. Squeak! Squeeeak! Squeeeeak!

"Well—it may not be a puppy—but it's something alive!" said Terry. "It doesn't really *sound* like a puppy—or a kitten either, really."

Tessie went to look out of the hall window. "The noise seems to come from outside somewhere," she said. "There—I heard it again!"

They listened eagerly. And then Tessie gave a heavy sigh and said "Oh!" in such a miserable voice that Terry was astonished. "What's the matter?" he said.

"Can't you see what's making the squeak?" said Tessie, disappointed. "Look—it's our back-gate! It's swinging to and fro in the wind, and squeaking each time."

"Horrible old gate!" said Terry, very disappointed too. "I'll go out and oil you this minute—pretending to be a puppy, and squeaking just like one!"

"Cheer up!" said Tessie. "It's our birthday tomorrow, and even if we *don't* get a kitten or a puppy, we'll have lots of other things. I vote we go to bed early tonight to make the birthday come quicker!"

"Well, if we don't get *some* pet between us tomorrow, I'll—I'll—well, I don't know *what* I'll do!" said Terry. "Something FIERCE!"

2. "AREN'T THERE ANY MORE PRESENTS?"

THE twins' mother came into their bedroom the next morning, and drew the curtains. "Happy birthday, twins!" she said. "Even the sun has decided to make it a nice day for you!"

She gave them each a birthday hug and a kiss. "All your presents are waiting for you downstairs," she said. "So I know you'll dress at top speed this morning! WHAT a good thing it's Saturday, and there's no school today! Well, well —to think you're nine years old—and in your tenth year already! You *are* growing up!"

The twins washed and dressed at top speed. As they dressed they heard the postman come. What a loud ratta-tat-TAT he gave! "He must have a lot of cards for us, and perhaps some parcels!" said Terry. "Oh, *where's* my other sock! I'm longing to go downstairs."

The postman had certainly brought them a lot of cards! Eight for each of them, and four between them as well. And there were four parcels besides, all looking very exciting in their brown paper.

On the breakfast table were other parcels, this time wrapped up in pretty birthday paper, not brown paper. "Hello, twins!" said Daddy, and gave them a birthday hug each. "Many happy returns of the day! How does it feel to be nine?"

"Well—no different from yesterday, really," said Terry. "I always *think* there'll be a difference, but there isn't. Mummy, may we open our parcels?"

"Two each before breakfast—and the rest afterwards," said his mother. The twins looked at the parcels. It was quite clear that none of them held a puppy or a kitten! But perhaps one was waiting outside! Once when they had had a tricycle given to them, it had been out in the yard. A puppy might quite well be out there too—in a box, or even a kennel!

They chose two big parcels and opened them in excitement.

"I *say*! Look at this ship!" said Terry, his eyes shining. "And I didn't even put it down on my list. Who gave it to me? OH! Isn't it a beauty. Daddy, may I sail it on the pond this afternoon?"

"I should think so," said Daddy. "Look, there's the card to say who gave it to you."

Terry looked at it. It said "Lots of love from

Daddy." He ran at his father and gave him a real bear-hug. "Daddy—*you* gave it to me. Oh, it's a beauty. Tom's got one too, but his is only half the size of this one. Oh, what shall I call it?"

"LOOK what I've got," said Tessie, suddenly. She had been undoing one of her biggest parcels too. "A doll's cot! Mummy, I know it's from you, I know it is! You said the other day that my baby doll ought to sleep in a cot! Oh, Mummy, it's lovely! I can buy some blankets and sheets and a pillow for it if I get any birthday money."

"Look and see what *Granny's* given you before you do that," said Mummy, and Tessie hurriedly undid the other big parcel.

"Oh, Granny's given me everything for the cot!" she said in delight. "Look Mummy—there's even a little eiderdown! Oh won't my baby doll be pleased?"

Terry had undone his second parcel now—and he couldn't for the life of him think what it was. It was a long curved piece of wood, smooth to the touch, and sharp at the edges.

"Oh—*I* know what it is!" he said. "It's that funny thing they throw in Australia—that comes back to your hand—what's it called now?"

"A boomerang," said Daddy. "Yes, Uncle

Roddy has sent it from Australia—he bought it specially for you. You'll be able to practise with it in the garden—throw it at one of the apple trees and knock off the ripest apple at the top!"

"You really must have your breakfast now," said Mummy. "Then you can open your other parcels. Sit down, twins."

The twins sat down to their boiled eggs, gazing at the ship, the boomerang, the doll's cot and the cot-clothes. What fun they were going to have with them—and there were still plenty of parcels to undo. Really, a birthday was very exciting!

But still at the back of their minds was a little worrying thought—*was* there going to be a puppy or kitten—or not? That would be much the nicest present of all—something alive, that they could love and that would love them. They listened for any bark or mew from outside—but they couldn't hear anything.

They opened the rest of their presents after breakfast. A magnificent new pencil-box for Tessie, filled with pencils, pens, crayons and two rubbers—an enormous jigsaw between them both —snap-cards for Terry—a book for each of them from Granpa—and hurrah, they were the books they wanted.

They opened the rest of their presents

"Mine's all about birds—the very one I was looking at in the book-shop the other day!" said Tessie. "Good old Granpa! It's a beauty! And oh —you've got the animal book *you* wanted, Terry. Bags I read it after you! What super pictures!"

There was a tin of toffees for each of them, a clockwork car for Terry, and a lovely little Spanish doll for Tessie.

"I know who she's from!" said Tessie, in delight. "Auntie Kate—because she went to Spain for her holiday and *told* me she'd brought back my birthday present from there! Mummy, I shall call this doll Juanita, and stand her on the mantelpiece, because she's good enough for an ornament! She's too smart to cuddle!"

The twins were really delighted with all their presents. They set them out on the floor and gloated over them.

"Clear up the paper and string, dears," said Mummy. "And I'll clear away the breakfast."

"Mummy—there aren't any *more* presents, are there?" asked Terry, still hopeful that there might be something alive, even if it was only a canary.

"Good gracious, dear—how many more do you want!" said Mummy, stacking the plates together. "You've been very, very lucky."

"There aren't any out in the yard this time, are there?" said Tessie. "You know—like our tricycle was once."

"*No*, darling," said Mummy. "You sound quite greedy! Now go and kiss Baby—she's not old enough to know it's your birthday, but you must kiss her all the same!"

The twins went off to the little room where Baby slept by herself. She was awake and kicking all the clothes off.

"We didn't have a puppy or a kitten after all," said Terry, mournfully, as they looked down at the smiling baby.

"I know—and I'm awfully disappointed that we haven't even got a canary," said Tessie. "I'd much rather have had that than that lovely doll's cot. Still—we've got Baby Anne—she's really *quite* a pet, isn't she?"

"Yes. She's a darling," said Terry. "And *she'd* love a puppy too, I know she would. Oh well—let's go and put our cards up round our bedrooms. We really have been very lucky, you know!"

*"OH QUICK—
DO SOMETHING!"*

THE twins enjoyed their birthday morning
very much. After they had done their
usual little jobs—making their beds,
sweeping and dusting their rooms, and running
Saturday errands for their mother, they were free
to play with their new toys.

"I'd really like to sail my ship," said Terry,
looking at it longingly. "I was going to sail it this
afternoon, but our party begins at half-past three,
doesn't it, Mummy?"

"Yes, dear—and you'll have to blow up the
balloons for me," said Mummy, "and bring some
bedroom chairs down for the dining-room because
we shan't have enough. And I want Tessie to pick
some flowers out of the garden and arrange them
in the vases for me, to make the rooms look nice."

"Mummy, we'll do all that, of course," said
Terry. "But it really won't take us long. Couldn't
we take my boat to sail on the pond this morning?"

"I want to make up my new doll's cot," said
Tessie. "It will be such fun to make the bed for the
first time and put that little pink eiderdown on

top. My baby doll is very, very pleased with it, Mummy!"

Mummy laughed. "I'm sure she is. Well, look now, why don't you do all my little jobs, and make your doll's cot up quickly—and then go to the pond with Terry? He really is longing to sail his ship. You'll want some string, Terry, because the pond is big, and if the wind blows hard, it might take your ship right out into the middle of the water."

"I've got some string," said Terry, patting his pocket. "Plenty. All right—we'll buck up and do everything, Mummy, and then go to the pond. Can we take Baby with us in her pram?"

"No. Not by the pond," said Mummy. "I do trust you, you know that—but it would be dreadful if the pram ran down into the pond. I'll keep Baby here."

It wasn't long before the twins had done everything, and Tessie had made up her new cot beautifully, and put the baby doll into it. She looked very peaceful, lying there with her eyes shut.

Baby Anne was in her pram, lying peacefully with *her* eyes shut too. Tessie wished they could take her to the pond—she did so like being with them. She picked up Baby's soft yellow duck, and put it near her hand.

"She loves it, but she's always throwing it away!" said Tessie. "I've picked it up about a hundred times, I should think! Are you ready, Terry? Is your new ship heavy to carry? It's so big!"

"I don't care how heavy it is," said Terry, proudly. "I *like* carrying it! Won't all the children stare when we meet them. Come on, Tessie."

The other children certainly did stare when they saw the big ship Terry was carrying. Harry came up and wanted to carry it for him. But Terry wouldn't let him. Nobody else was going to carry his birthday ship that day!

It was quite a long way to the pond. They had to go up the hill and down again, round a corner, and then, lying at the edge of the field, there was the pond.

It was a nice big one, and it usually had ducks on it, but this morning there were none. It was fairly deep in the middle, and would have been nicer if only people hadn't thrown rubbish into it. There was a tin kettle, two old cans and a wooden box that bobbed up and down. They spoilt the pretty little pond.

"Well, now we'll see how my new ship sails!" said Terry, in delight. "I've decided to call her *Flying Swan*, Tessie. Do you think that's a good name?"

"Oh *yes*," said Tessie. "Ships do look rather like swans when they're sailing. It's a nice name."

Soon the ship was on the pond. It floated beautifully, and didn't flop on its side at all, as some ships do.

"Look at her!" said Terry, in delight. "See how she bobs over the little ripples! Look how the wind is filling her sails just like a real ship! She's speeding over the water exactly like those ships we saw down at the seaside."

The ship really was a fine sight to watch. She sailed over the pond right to the very end of her string, and then, when Terry pulled at her gently, she turned and came back again, as steady as could be!

"Let me hold her now," said Tessie, and Terry gave her the string. Tessie liked to feel the ship pulling at her hand as she sailed here and there. "She feels alive when the string pulls on my finger," she said. "Oh look, Terry—is one of her sails coming loose? Yes, look—it's gone all crooked."

"Let me have the string," said Terry at once. "I expect a knot has come loose." He took the string from Tessie, and pulled the boat in carefully.

"Yes—it's just a knot that wants tying up," he said. "Let's go and sit down by that bush and I can do it properly."

So they took the ship to the big bush and sat down. The knot was very awkward to tie, and the two children bent their heads over the ship, lost in what they were doing.

They didn't see a big boy come up and look all round. He didn't see them either, for the bush hid them, and they were not making a sound. He carried a small parcel, something tied up in an old flour bag. He had it hidden under his jacket.

He didn't come right down to the pond, but stood a little way away, still looking cautiously all round. Then he raised his arm and threw the flour bag straight over the water of the pond.

"SPLASH!"

The noise made the twins lift their heads at once and stare at the pond. "What was that?" asked Terry. "What fell into the water just then?"

"I don't know," said Tessie, puzzled. "I didn't see anything. And there's nobody about. Perhaps it was a fish or a frog jumping."

"Look—what's that over there—in the middle of the pond?" said Terry. "It's something moving. Whatever can it be?"

Then a noise came to their ears—a high-pitched squeak, and the thing in the pond began to roll over and over.

"Look—see that bag, or whatever it is?" said Terry, leaping up. "That's what fell—or was thrown in—and there's something in it, Tessie! Something alive!"

"Oh quick, then do something!" cried Tessie. "It will drown! See how it's struggling—but it can't get out of the bag!"

Terry tore off his shoes and socks and waded into the water. The bottom of the pond was muddy and his feet sank into it as he waded. The water soon came over his

What could it be?

knees—but at last he managed to reach out to
the struggling thing near him, and picked it up.
At once he felt a wriggling, frantic little body
inside. What could it be? What *could* it be?

"TESSIE! There's something inside this
bag!" cried Terry. "It feels like some tiny
animal. Oh, how *could* anyone do such a
cruel thing! Fancy tying it up and then throwing it
away to drown!"

He waded to shore, holding the wriggling little
thing in the bag as gently as he could. It struggled
and squeaked in terror.

"What is it? Oh, Terry, poor little thing! Undo
the knots tying up the bag!" cried Tessie. "Who
threw it into the pond? I never saw anyone come—
I only heard the splash."

"I can't undo these knots," said Terry, sitting
down to try again. "The string is so wet. Put your
hand into my left-hand pocket. Tessie, and get
out my knife for me."

Tessie did as she was told, and handed him his
knife, opening the blade for him first. He took it
and cut the string. The mouth of the old flour bag
fell open—and a tiny white tail appeared.

"Look—there's its tail!" said Tessie. "What a
tiny creature—no bigger than a rat. It isn't a

white rat, is it, Terry? Be careful the poor thing doesn't bite you."

"I'll take it out very carefully," said Terry. "It's so terrified—and so weak too, now. I expect it's half-drowned!"

Very gently indeed he pulled the tiny creature out of the dripping wet bag. At first the children couldn't make out what it was, it was so wet and draggled and small. Then a tiny mew came from the little thing, and they both knew at once what it was.

"A *kitten!* A tiny, tiny kitten," said Tessie. "A white one. Oh, poor little thing, it's so frightened. It can't be more than two or three weeks old. Has it got its eyes open? It's so wet and miserable, I can't see."

"We'd better take it home and dry it at once," said Terry. "It ought to be put somewhere warm, it's shivering. What a pity the sun's just gone in! Oh, poor little frightened thing, we'll do what we can for you!"

"Give it to me," said Tessie. "I'll dry it gently with my hanky—and then I'll put it inside my jersey and hold it there. It will be warm then. What a tiny, tiny mew it has!"

Terry gave the kitten to her, and watched his

sister dry the little thing with her handkerchief. It didn't seem to like it much, and mewed again. But it liked it when Tessie put it carefully under her soft woollen jersey and held it there safely. It stopped mewing at once.

"You get your ship," said Tessie. "We left it there, by the bush. You don't want to sail it any more, do you?"

"No," said Terry. "I want to get this kitten home and safe. What do you think Mummy will say, Tessie?"

Tessie was silent. What *would* Mummy say? She didn't want pets in the house while she had Baby to carry about, up and down stairs; and certainly it would be dreadful if she fell over a kitten on the stairs, with Baby in her arms. But how could they do anything but take it home?

"We can't tell Mummy *today*,"

"What a tiny mew!"

said Terry. "She has a lot to do, because it's our birthday, and there's our party this afternoon."

"Well—where can we put the kitten then?" said Tessie. "Not in the house, because Mummy would hear it squeaking. It would have to be somewhere outside."

"Let's put it in the old shed," said Terry. "Nobody ever goes there except us, now Daddy has built a new shed. There's only just our tricycles there, and our old spades and things. We could make a bed for the kitten there."

"What about feeding it?" said Tessie. "How do we feed it? How old is it, I wonder? Its mother still ought to be feeding it, oughtn't she? Oh dear—what a lot of difficulties there are!"

"Isn't there anyone we can ask?" wondered Terry. "Someone who knows about animals? We've never had any, so we really don't know. What about Harry? His father is an animal doctor, isn't he? What's he called now—a vet?"

"Yes," said Tessie. "A vet. He went to Farmer Hill when his horses were ill—and he mended the leg of Mrs. Brown's dog, when he got run over—and he took a thorn out of Hilary's cat's front paw. I was there when he did that. He's nice. Yes, let's ask Harry if he knows anything about tiny kittens."

"Well—if *my* father was an animal doctor, I'd know a lot about animals!" said Terry. "I'd love to learn. Let's go to Harry's house and see if he's in."

So they went to Harry Williams' house and walked round the back to find him. Terry was still carrying his big ship, of course, and Tessie had the kitten cuddled under her jersey. It had stopped squeaking now, because it was beginning to feel warm.

Harry was playing in his garden. "Hallo!" he said, in surprise. "What have you come for—to show me that ship? My word, isn't it a real beauty?"

"No. We came to ask if you knew anything about tiny kittens," said Terry. "Someone threw one into the pond when we were there with my ship—and I waded in and got it. It's so wet and cold and miserable. We thought perhaps you'd know how we could feed it."

"No, *I* don't," said Harry. "But the kennel-maid who helps my father with the dogs here would tell you."

"Will you ask her?" said Tessie.

A sly look came into Harry's eyes. "Yes—if you lend me your ship to sail," he said.

"I can't do that!" said Terry. "I only had it to-day, for my birthday!"

"Well, I shan't ask the kennel-maid for you, then," said Harry. "Why don't you ask your mother? She'd know."

"She doesn't want us to have animals yet, till our baby is bigger," explained Tessie. "Harry, don't be mean—the tiny thing is so frightened and miserable. We simply *must* get advice."

"Well, tell Terry to lend me his ship and I'll go straight and ask the kennel-maid," said Harry.

Terry gave Harry the ship when he saw Tessie's

"Lend me your ship to sail"

eyes filling with tears. He never could bear to see his twin sister upset. "All right. Here you are," he said. "But you're *mean*. I shall get into a row with my father if he finds I've lent my ship to someone. Now go and ask the kennel-maid."

"You come with me," said Harry, taking the big ship in delight. "My word—isn't she a beauty? Has she a name?"

"The *Flying Swan*," said Terry, in an angry voice. He thought Harry was really horrid.

"Pooh—what a silly name! I shall call her *Snow-Maiden*," said Harry.

"You won't! She's *my* ship," said Terry, but Harry only laughed. "Come on—bring the kitten," he said. "What a lot of fuss you make about a silly half-drowned creature! Look — there's Miss Morgan, the kennel-maid. Go and ask her what you want to!" And off he ran—carrying Terry's lovely ship with him!

"PLEASE TELL
US WHAT TO DO"

MISS Morgan, the kennel-maid, was very busy. She had four dogs on leads, and was putting them into their kennels. She talked to them as she shut them in.

"Now you be good, all of you—and Tinker, it's no use your barking the place down, you'll only upset the others. I'll take you all for another run this afternoon if you're quiet. And don't you try and bite that bandage off your leg, Lassie—be a good dog now!"

The twins waited until she had shut up all the dogs safely. They thought she sounded sensible and kind, and when she turned round they saw that she had a merry, smiling face.

"Hallo!" she said. "What do *you* want? Have you come to see the vet? He's out."

"No. We came to see Harry really," said Terry, "to ask him if he knew what we could do to help a half-drowned kitten—and he said we could ask *you* for advice."

"A half-drowned kitten—whatever have you been doing to the poor thing?" said Miss Morgan, as Tessie drew it gently out from the warmth of her jersey.

"Nothing!" said Terry. "*We* didn't try to drown it! Someone came to the pond when we were sailing our ship and threw a bag into the water—and we saw the bag wriggling—and I waded out to it . . ."

She shut up all the dogs safely

"And when we undid the bag, there was this tiny wet kitten inside, choking and spluttering," said Tessie. "It was so frightened and cold."

"Poor wee thing," said Miss Morgan, and took it gently from Tessie's hands. "It's in a bad way. It's been half-starved by the look of it—and see, there's something wrong with one of its back legs."

"PLEASE tell us what to do with it," said Tessie, in tears. "Will it live?"

"Oh yes, I think so," said Miss Morgan. "It's not shivering now—and by the sound of its little mew, it's very hungry. I'll show you how to feed it."

She took them into the little bare surgery, where the vet saw all his animal patients, and went to a cupboard. She handed Terry a small fountain-pen filler. "There's some warm milk in that saucepan over there," she said. "I've been feeding a puppy with it, but there's enough left for this tiny mite. Put some in the glass filler, will you?"

Terry put the glass end of the filler into the saucepan of milk, squeezed the rubber end, and drew milk into the filler. Miss Morgan took it from him.

"Open your mouth, kitty," she said, and put the filler gently against the kitten's mouth. A drop of milk ran in, and the kitten swallowed it. It mewed.

"Yes—it liked that," said Miss Morgan. "Well, take a few more drops, kitty—you'll soon feel better!"

The twins watched Miss Morgan feeding the tiny creature, and were delighted to see how eagerly it swallowed the milk. Terry filled the little pen-filler twice more, and was allowed to feed the kitten himself. Then Tessie had a turn.

"Well, that's how you must feed it, until it can lap," said Miss Morgan. "Have you a filler at home? I can give you one if you haven't."

"Yes, Tessie's got one," said Terry. "How shall we know when the kitten is ready to lap, Miss Morgan?"

"It will lick a drop of milk off your finger then," said Miss Morgan. "As soon as it does that, you can teach it to lap from a saucer. It will soon learn!"

"Its eyes aren't open," said Tessie. "Is it very, very young?"

"It's very, very *small*," said Miss Morgan, "small enough for its eyes still not to be open—but I think it's older than it looks. I expect it hasn't opened its eyes because it's weak and neglected. Are you sure you can look after it?"

The twins nodded. "Yes!" said Terry. "We can—we mean to, anyway. Who else would, if we didn't?"

"What about its leg?" asked Tessie, anxiously.

"The leg that hangs limp and doesn't move."

"I think that will get all right," said Miss Morgan. "But if not, you can bring it back to me again. Now—keep the kitten somewhere warm—it will probably have felt shocked and chilled, when it struggled in the cold pond water! I'm glad you were there to save it."

She gave the tiny thing to Tessie, who put it back under her warm jersey again. "It's more like a white rat than a kitten!" said Miss Morgan. "But it should grow up into a pretty little thing. Take it home now."

"Do we—do we have to pay you anything for helping us?" asked Terry. "I did lend Harry my birthday ship, but you've done such a lot. We've got some birthday money you could have."

"Bless you!" said Miss Morgan, smiling her nice smile. "I'm glad to help, and there isn't even a penny to pay. It's your birthday, is it? Many happy returns of the day! You've had a very unexpected birthday present, haven't you—a half-drowned kitten!"

The twins set off down the path. "She's nice, isn't she?" said Tessie. "Let's buy her some sweets sometime. I feel better about the kitten now, don't you? If it can take milk so easily it will soon be all right. It feels so nice against me, under my jersey."

"Tessie—do you think we'd *better* put it into the shed while it's so tiny?" asked Terry, as they walked off down the road. "And don't you think we ought to give it milk in the middle of the night? You know, Mother gives Baby her bottle quite a lot of times, doesn't she, morning, after-noon and night—and *early* in the morning too!"

"Well—we can't possibly creep out of the house in the middle of the night to feed the kitten," said Tessie.

"No, we can't," said Terry. "Perhaps we'd better find somewhere near our bedrooms. What about the little boxroom? If the kitten made a noise no one would hear it there—and it's next to our bedrooms."

"Yes. We could keep it there till it doesn't need feeding at night," said Tessie, cheering up. "Oh dear—I DO wish we could tell Mummy about it. Can't we possibly?"

"No. It would be mean of us to ask her to do something on our birthday that she's already re-fused to do," said Terry. "She might think she'd *got* to have the kitten, and then it would be a nuisance instead of something lovely. I think we can manage all right, Tessie."

"But what about when it grows big?" said Tessie.

"Don't let's bother about that yet," said Terry. "We could give it away, I expect. The thing is we've got to be kind to it *now*, and get it well and happy. Here we are—now be careful nobody sees us, and asks you what that bump is under your jumper!"

They went quietly to the back door and peeped in. Nobody was there. They tiptoed in, and went quietly up the stairs. "We'll go straight to the box-room," whispered Terry.

And then they heard Mummy's voice! "Is that you, twins? I wondered whatever had happened to you! Come and tell me what you've been doing this birthday morning!"

"WHAT A GOOD IDEA!"

THE twins looked at one another in dismay, and Tessie clutched the kitten more closely to her, hoping it would not make the tiniest sound.

"You pop upstairs quickly," said Terry, "and find a place to put the kitten. I'll go in and talk to Mummy."

Tessie raced upstairs. She went into the tiny boxroom. The hot-water pipes ran through it, so it was nice and warm. "Just the place for a cold little kitten!" thought Tessie. "Now—what shall I give it for a bed?"

There was nowhere in the boxroom that would be soft and comfortable. Tessie wondered what to use for a cosy little bed—and then she suddenly thought of something. Yes! Her new doll's cot! It would be just the right size for the kitten.

She ran into the playroom. The cot stood beside the toy cupboard, and the little baby doll was lying in it, with her eyes closed. Tessie lifted her out and put her on a chair.

"This will be just right for you, kitten!" she said, and went back into the little boxroom with the cot. She set it down in a corner and turned back the cot-clothes. She took out the sheets and left the little blanket, the pillow and the pink eiderdown. She put the tiny kitten on to the blanket and covered it up with the eiderdown.

"There!" she said. "Now you lie there and sleep, kitten—and don't make any noise! You'll be quite safe here, because nobody ever comes into this room."

She heard footsteps running up the stairs. It was Terry. "Tessie —where are you? Is everything all right?"

"Yes—come and look!" said Tessie, and took Terry into the boxroom. He laughed when he saw the tiny kitten in the cot.

"What a good idea! But that won't be big enough for it when it gets older. It could have my

"It's fast asleep"

toy garage then, with a blanket inside—or the brick-box!"

"It's fast asleep," said Tessie. "It's quite dry now—look, its fur is beginning to look nice and soft. How *could* anyone throw such a dear little thing away?"

"When do you think we ought to feed it again?" asked Terry. "It's almost dinner-time now for us. Shall we feed it afterwards?"

"Yes. Baby always leaves a little warm milk in her bottle," said Tessie. "We can use that. Where's that little glass filler of mine?"

"I saw it in your old pencil-box," said Terry. "I'll go and look. We'd better keep the boxroom door shut, Tessie, in case anyone hears the little thing mewing."

They went down to their dinner. It was nice to have a secret, but it would have been nicer still to share it with Mummy and Daddy!

"Well, birthday children!" said Daddy. "Are you looking forward to your party? I see there is a magnificent cake out in the kitchen!"

"Yes—with eighteen candles on it!" said Tessie. "Goodness—when we're eighteen, there'll have to be thirty-six, won't there, Mummy?"

After dinner Mummy had to give Baby her

bottle. "Shall I give it to her for you, Mummy?" asked Tessie. "I know you're busy. I've fed her before, so you know you can trust me."

"All right—you may if you're very careful," said Mummy. "I'll get Baby for you, and settle her on your knee, and then prepare her bottle."

So, very soon, there was Tessie sitting in Mummy's low nursing-chair, proudly giving Baby Anne her bottle! Terry came to see. "If she leaves any milk, let me have it for the kitten," he said. "It will be nice and warm."

"Well, get the milk jug from my dolls' tea-set," said Tessie. "I can pour it quickly in there, when Baby has finished."

Terry fetched the little jug. Baby seemed very hungry and was sucking at her bottle vigorously. Mummy popped her head in at the door to see that everything was all right.

"Dear me—she's almost finished her bottle!" she said. "Don't bother her to finish the last few drops if she doesn't want them. Can you put her back into her cot for me and play with her for a bit till I'm ready for her?"

"Yes, I will," said Tessie. Mummy was right— Baby didn't want the last few drops, and Terry took off the bottle-teat and trickled the drops of milk into the little dolls' jug he had fetched.

"I'll go up to the kitten now," he said. "You come as soon as Mummy fetches Baby."

He ran upstairs with the little jug, and went cautiously into the boxroom. The kitten was still in the cot, but it was squirming about, wide awake, although its eyes were still fast shut.

Terry picked it up carefully, sat down on the floor, and set the tiny thing in the hollow of his crossed legs. Then he tried to feed it just as the kennel-maid had shown him. But the kitten was more lively now, and didn't seem to know that there was milk about. Terry was very glad when Tessie came up to join him.

"You hold the kitten in your hands and I'll try and open its mouth enough to get the end of the filler in," she said. And before long the kitten was eagerly drinking down the warm drops of milk that fell into its tiny mouth from the end of the glass filler.

"Goodness—isn't it hungry again!" said Terry. "I don't think it will be able to wait till Baby has her bottle at six o'clock!"

"Well, I've thought what we can do," said Tessie. "I'll go down to the kitchen and get a little milk out of the larder. And we'll keep it up here, touching the hot-water pipe, so that it will always be warm. And then we can pop in here whenever we have a minute to see if the kitten would like a meal."

"That's an *awfully* good idea!" said Terry.

The kitten was eagerly drinking

"There—the kitten's finished every drop of milk we brought up for it."

"Mummy's calling us," said Tessie. "I expect she wants us to get ready for the party. It begins at half past three, you know. I'll tuck the kitten up, and then we'll go down. And if either of us has a chance to slip up here in the middle of the party to give the kitten a drink, we will."

"You run and get some milk out of the larder,

while I go to help Mummy," said Terry. "Leave it just there, by that hot-water pipe."

He ran downstairs, and Tessie followed. She heard him talking to Mummy, and went into the kitchen. She took a small cup from the dresser and poured a little milk into it from the milk-jug. She shut the larder door carefully, and went slowly upstairs with the cup, careful not to spill even a drop.

"Here I am again, kitten!" she said, and put the cup against the hot-water pipe. "Oh—you're asleep! You do look sweet with your head on the pillow—you look like a toy kitten, not a real one!"

Then down she went to get ready for the party. What an exciting day this was!

THE party began at half past three, when boys and girls began to come up the path to the front door. The boys looked very clean and tidy, and the girls very gay in their frilly party frocks. The twins gave them a great welcome.

"It's a pity we asked Harry to the party," said Terry to Tessie, as they saw Harry coming up to the door.

"Yes—but we didn't know he was going to be so mean," said Tessie.

"How's the kitten?" said Harry, as he came up to them.

"All right. And we haven't said anything about it yet, so don't *you* say anything either," said Terry, afraid that Harry would give away their secret.

Then someone else came, and the twins had to leave Harry. Bother him! He had their ship—and their secret as well!

The party was lovely. All the children brought little presents of sweets or chocolates, and admired the lovely things that the twins had had given them. Terry did hope that Mummy wouldn't notice his big ship wasn't among them! Whatever should he say if she asked him where it was.

But she didn't. She was much too busy taking coats and hats, and then starting off the games with "Here we come gathering nuts in May!" to bother about anything else! What fun a party was!

How exciting the tea was too! Mummy had made four different kinds of sandwiches, three different kinds of cakes besides the big birthday cake, and little wobbly jellies for everyone. It was a great moment when the candles on the big cake were lighted.

"Gracious! *Eighteen!*" said little Kenneth. "Are you eighteen years old? You don't look it!"

"*How's the kitten?*"

"Don't you know your twice times table yet?" said Harry. "Twice times nine are eighteen! The twins are nine today. Baby!"

After tea Mummy asked if anyone wanted to wash their hands. "You take them up-stairs if they do," she said to the twins. "Then we'll play some more games."

"Tessie—now's our chance to feed the kitten again!" said Terry in a low voice. "I'll do it, shall I?"

Tessie nodded. "Yes—but don't be too long. The filler is in the cup, standing by the hot-water pipe."

Terry sped off to the little boxroom. He went in and shut the door. The kitten was squirming about in the dolls' cot, giving very small mews.

"Just coming!" Terry said to it, and went to where Tessie had stood the cup of milk by the hot pipe. He drew some into the little filler and went over to the cot. The kitten smelt the warm milk at once and mewed quite loudly. It swallowed drop after drop as Terry squeezed them out of the filler, into its tiny mouth.

"You're getting quite used to this performance, aren't you!" he said. "There! That's enough, I should think. Now I must get back to the party."

He joined the others, and gave Tessie a little nod that meant: "Yes—the kitten's fed!" and she smiled. The little creature had been at the back of her mind all the afternoon.

The party began again with musical chairs and then hunt the thimble, and then a treasure hunt, which was very exciting. Every child was given the end of a long thread and told to follow it to the other end, where he or she would find a present—but very soon the threads began to get tangled up, and then the fun began!

"I think you've all found the wrong presents!" said the twins' mother, laughing at the muddle. "But never mind—you can change presents if you like!"

Nobody wanted to go when mothers and fathers arrived to fetch their boys and girls. Soon there was only Harry left. He was always last at parties, and as no one ever fetched him, he was very difficult to get rid of! Terry was afraid he would begin to talk about the ship, and he went off and left him with Tessie.

"I must go and help Mummy with Baby," said Tessie, firmly. "Good-bye, Harry. I hope you enjoyed the party."

"Well, you didn't have fruit salad," said Harry. "And I do like fruit salad."

That was so like Harry! He went off at last and didn't even say "Thank you for a lovely time!" as all the others did.

Soon the threads began to get tangled up

Tessie flew up to the boxroom calling out to her mother that she wouldn't be a minute. Terry was already there, having just given the kitten another meal of warm milk.

"Oh good!" said Tessie. "It looks quite happy now, doesn't it, Terry. Do you think it's forgotten the shock it had this morning, when it was thrown into the pond?"

"I expect so," said Terry. "It wasn't in the water long, anyway. Mummy's calling you, Tessie. I say—wasn't it a grand party?"

"Yes, wonderful!" said Tessie, rushing off to help her mother.

"Would you like to feed Baby for me again?" said Mother. "I've rather a lot of washing up to do, and Baby is always so good with you. You do like feeding her, don't you?"

"Oh yes—feeding babies and kittens is lovely," said Tessie, before she could stop herself. Mummy was surprised.

"What do *you* know about feeding kittens?" she said, and went off to do the washing up.

"Goodness—I nearly gave our secret away!" thought Tessie. "What a good thing Terry didn't hear me—he *would* have been cross! All the same I'm sure Mummy would agree with me, if she could see our tiny kitten!"

"Well, did you enjoy your birthday?" asked Mummy, when Baby was safely in her cot again, and it was time for the twins to go to bed. Tessie gave her mother a hug.

"It was *lovely*!" she said. "From the time we woke up till this very minute. Thank you for a fine party too, Mummy—and *wasn't* our cake delicious!"

"It seemed to be," said Terry. "Harry had four pieces!"

"Go and say good night to Daddy," said Mummy, "and take some milk and biscuits up to bed with you for your supper. I'm sure you won't want anything more than that tonight, after your enormous tea!"

The twins looked at one another when she said "milk" and they both thought the same thing. They could save some for the kitten.

"What did you like best at the party?" asked Terry, as they went upstairs with their supper.

"Blowing all the eighteen candles out at once!" said Tessie. "I never thought we should! Now— just let's give the kitten its supper—and then it won't get any more until one of us wakes up in the night and goes to feed it. I hope we do—it will be so very hungry in the morning, if not!"

"WE HAVEN'T GIVEN IT A NAME YET"

THE twins found the kitten fast asleep, and had to wake it to give it its "supper". It mewed as soon as it smelt the milk again. Terry stroked its soft fur.

"It was such an ugly little thing this morning," he said. "All wet and draggled—now it's sweet— but awfully thin. And I wish its back leg wasn't useless. It doesn't seem able to use it at all, when it tries to crawl."

"Perhaps that's one reason why it was thrown away," said Tessie. "Perhaps the owner didn't want to be bothered by a crippled kitten. How would *he* like it if he broke a leg or arm, and was thrown into a pond to drown, instead of being looked after in hospital till he was better!"

"Better buck up, Tessie," said Terry, "or Mummy will be up before we've undressed! Now —if either of us wakes in the night, we feed the kitten. Have you got your torch handy, because you mustn't switch on any lights? We might wake Mummy or Daddy if we do."

"We'll each slip our torches under our pillow,"

said Tessie. "Goodness me, kitten, surely you can't take any more milk! No—it's had enough now. I'll tuck it up again. I think it knows us already, don't you, Terry?"

"Well—it knows the milk-dropper all right!" said Terry, with a grin. "Give me the cup—I'll stand it by the hot pipe again. That was a brilliant idea of yours, Tessie—it just warms the milk nicely."

The twins were tired after their exciting day, and once they were in bed, they were soon asleep. Terry didn't wake once in the night—but Tessie did! She sat up in bed. Now—what had she got to remember if she woke up—oh yes—that kitten, of course.

It seemed strange in the dark little boxroom

And out of bed she slipped with her torch, and was soon cuddling the mewing kitten and feeding it with drops of milk. It seemed strange to be sitting there in the dark little boxroom, with the light from the torch streaking across the floor where she had laid it down.

"I wish I could take you into bed with me and keep you warm," she said to the kitten. "There— I'll tuck you up in the cot again. I wonder if you miss your mother. I expect she's missing *you*, and wondering where you've gone."

Terry was quite upset because he hadn't awakened in the night. They both marvelled at the kitten in the morning, because it seemed bigger already.

"I believe one of its eyes is trying to open!" said Tessie, looking at it closely. "Yes, it *is*—look, Terry—can you see a crack between its eyelids— the right eye, see?"

"Yes—it *is* opening!" said Terry. "Do you suppose it will have pink eyes, because it's a *white* kitten, Tessie? When we kept white mice, they all had pink eyes—do you remember?"

"Yes. But I don't much like pink eyes," said Tessie. "I want it to have green eyes."

"No—*blue*," said Terry. "A white kitten with

blue eyes would be lovely. Come on—we'd better go down. Mummy will soon be wondering why we keep disappearing!"

It was a good thing that it was holiday time because the twins would never have been able to feed the kitten as often as they did, if they had had to go to school each day. As it was, they had to take it out of the boxroom when a few days had gone by, because Mother suddenly said that she was going to turn out the little room and clean it.

"Turn it out?" said Tessie, startled. "But why, Mummy? It isn't untidy in there or anything, is it?"

"No. But I believe there are mice there," said Mummy. "I keep hearing little squeaks or something up on that landing, and the only place they can come from is the boxroom. I expect some mice have made a nest there of paper. I shall turn it out thoroughly tomorrow."

The twins had to make new plans for the kitten at once.

"The shed!" said Terry. "That's the only place that's safe. No one goes there but us, now Daddy has his new shed. I'll go out in the garden, Tessie, and if the coast is clear I'll whistle loudly. Then you can bring the kitten down at once. Wrap it up in a doll's shawl or something, then it will look as if it's a doll!"

Tessie ran up to the boxroom and wrapped the kitten in a little shawl. Then she heard Terry's whistle and ran downstairs. They got to the shed safely without being seen.

"Look—there's a little box here," said Terry. "Can you spare the shawl for a blanket? We could put some hay in the box under the shawl to make a nice soft bed. Did you bring the cup of

milk? We shan't be able to warm it by hot-water pipes now—but perhaps it won't matter now the kitten is getting bigger."

Both the kitten's eyes were open now. They were a pale blue, and the children hoped they wouldn't turn pink. It knew them well now, and had sud-

They got to the shed   denly found that it

could purr! The twins were surprised when they first heard it.

"Is it feeling ill? Why is it making that funny noise?" said Tessie, anxiously.

"Silly! It's *purring* for the first time!" said Terry. "That means it's happy. What a dear little noise!"

It was beginning to crawl about too, though it still dragged one back leg behind it. Tessie felt the leg gently, but it didn't seem to be broken. Perhaps it would get right.

It was a good thing that Tessie had taken the kitten out of the boxroom straight away—because Mummy changed her mind and turned it out that very morning.

"But I didn't find any mice!" she said. "All the same I found something rather *peculiar* in the box-room."

"What?" asked the twins.

"Your new dolls' cot, Tessie!" said Mummy. "Whatever was it doing in there? Did your baby doll cry at night and wake you—and so you put her there?"

That made the twins laugh. Terry changed the subject, afraid that Tessie wouldn't be able to explain about the dolls' cot and would go red, and make Mummy curious. They *couldn't* let the kitten be given away to anyone now—they really couldn't. And Mummy might say it would have to go, if she found out about it. But how could *anyone* help liking it—it really was the prettiest little thing now.

The days went by, and the kitten still lived in the shed, and the twins still fed it regularly. Once or twice they gave it bits of fish they had saved from their own dinner, and it gobbled them up. It had two rows of very small, pointed teeth, and big blue eyes.

"They're going to turn green, I think," said Terry. "It will be a lovely cat then—pure white with bright green eyes!"

"You know—we've never given it a name yet," said Tessie, rolling it over and over, and tickling its tummy. "What shall we call it?"

"I don't know," said Terry. "It's got fine whiskers—shall we call it Whiskers? Or Purry because it's always purring?"

"No. Those aren't *very* good names," said Tessie. "Oh, look at it—it's rolled itself up into a white ball, and it's fighting its tail. It's like a round ball of snow!"

"*That's* its name—Snowy!" said Terry, at once. "Snowy—you'll have to learn your name! Snowy!"

"Miaow!" said Snowy, and ran to Terry.

"There!" he said. "You know your name already, don't you, Snowy?"

"YOU'RE THE MEANEST BOY IN THE WORLD"

THAT Saturday something very awkward happened. Daddy announced that he would like to sail Terry's birthday ship with him!

"We'll take it down to the pond," he said. "There's a little breeze and the ship would sail well."

But *Harry* still had the ship! He wouldn't give it back, though Terry had asked him many times.

"No," he said, each time. "As long as I keep your secret about the kitten, you've got to lend me your ship. If you take it back I'll tell about the kitten."

"You're horrible and mean and unkind," said Terry. He didn't like to see Tessie looking so troubled. But Harry only laughed.

And oh dear—now Daddy wanted to go and sail the ship that very afternoon!

Terry hunted about in his mind for some good excuse.

"Oh Daddy—it's a long way to the pond, and it looks like rain," he said, going very red.

"And Mummy asked me to take Baby in her

pram to see Granny," said Tessie, quite truthfully.

"Well, *you* can take Baby, and Terry can come with me," said Daddy. "A long way to the pond! I never heard such nonsense! Don't you *want* to come, Terry?"

"Oh *yes*!" said poor Terry. "I love going anywhere with you, Daddy, you know that!"

"Well, we'll go then," said Daddy. "Go and get your ship, and we'll have a look at her, and see if she's properly rigged."

Terry looked at Tessie in despair. Harry had the ship, so he couldn't *possibly* go and get it. Daddy was puzzled.

"Well, Terry, please go along and get it," he said, sounding impatient. "I should have thought you'd have loved the chance of sailing that lovely ship. I don't believe you've sailed it more than once, have you? I must say I've been rather surprised."

Terry didn't know what to do. He turned as if to go and get his ship. Tessie looked frightened, because she was sure that Daddy was soon going to be very angry!

Terry turned round again, his face as red as fire. "I can't go and get it, Daddy," he said. "It's not here."

"Well, where is it, then?" said Daddy, astonished.

"Er—I lent it to Harry—you know, the vet's son," stammered Terry. "He—he loves ships too."

"You lent that beautiful ship to *Harry*—that careless fellow!" cried his father. "Whatever possessed you to do that! Go and get it back at once."

"Well—you see," began Terry, and then didn't say any more, because that would have meant giving away the secret of the little white kitten. He stared miserably at his father.

"Well, either *you* go and get your ship back, or *I* go and get it," said Daddy. "And if *I* get it, I shall tell Master Harry what I think of him, for borrowing that beautiful ship. I told him he was *not* to borrow anything more from you, after he left those beautiful animal books of yours out in the rain all night."

"I'll go and get the ship," said Terry, at once. Harry would certainly give away the secret if Daddy went! He set off at once, hoping that Harry would not be mean. After all, he had had that lovely ship for ages now!

Harry *was* mean!

"You said I could have your ship as long as I

kept your secret," he said. "And I'm *still* keeping your secret, so I shall still keep your ship. Of course, if you don't *want* me to keep your secret any longer, I won't."

Terry stared at him, clenching his fists. He wanted to fight Harry at that moment. Harry saw the clenched fists and laughed.

"Of course, you can have your ship just for today, but you'll have to pay me fifty pence."

"You're the meanest boy in the whole world," said Terry, fiercely. He put his hand in his pocket and took out the Saturday money that his father had given him that morning. He slammed it down on the top of the wall.

"There you are! There's your money —now give me my ship!"

Harry moved towards the money, but Terry clapped his hand over it.

"No, you don't! You won't *touch*

"*Pay me fifty pence*"

my fifty pence until I have my ship," he said.

Harry laughed and went into his house. He brought out the ship and handed it to Terry, snatching the money as he did so.

"You've tangled up all the rigging," said Terry angrily. "And you've dented the keel."

"That was done when you lent it to me," said Harry at once.

"Fibber!" said Terry, disgusted, and went off with his ship. How he detested Harry! Just because he and Tessie had wanted help for a half-drowned kitten, Harry had got him into all this trouble. Whatever would Daddy say when he saw the tangled rigging and bent keel?

Daddy had a great deal to say about the ship! He was very cross indeed.

"To think you've let this lovely ship get into this state in such a short time!" he said. "Or did Harry do it? Yes, I suppose he did. Why in the world you lent it to him I don't know! You know I don't like you to have much to do with Harry—he's not a good friend for you. I'm very disappointed in you, Terry. I'm afraid it will take so long to get the ship ready for sailing that it's not worth while our going."

Terry couldn't bear to have his father so

disappointed in him. "I'm very sorry, Daddy," he said.

"Well, look—go and buy some new string, and we'll rig the whole ship again," said Daddy. "I gave you your fifty pence piece this morning, didn't I?"

Terry put his hand into his pocket—and then remembered that he had given it to Harry, so that he might get his ship back. Good gracious! Now he couldn't even buy the string.

"Now don't say you've spent all your money already," said Daddy. "You know you're supposed to save ten pence a week in your money box. Have you put that into it?"

"No, Daddy," said Terry.

"Well, do you mean to say you've spent it all?" said Daddy. "Not even a penny left?"

"I've got a penny from last week," said Terry, desperately, and took it out. He simply didn't know *what* to say.

Tessie had been listening to all this, frightened and unhappy. She went to Terry, holding out her own fifty pence.

"Terry can have *my* money," she said. "I've plenty in my money box. You go and buy the string, Terry."

"No," said Daddy, giving the ship back to Terry. "No. I don't feel as if I want to take Terry out with me today. I feel rather ashamed of him." And he went indoors without another word.

Poor Terry. He stared at Tessie, and then, afraid that he might cry, he rushed into the little shed, almost falling over Snowy the kitten. "What a thing to happen!" he said to the surprised kitten. "NOW what am I to do?"

DADDY wasn't at all pleased with Terry all that day and for several days afterwards. Mummy heard about the spoilt ship too, and was sad to think that Terry had lent it to Harry.

"I should have thought that you valued it too much to lend it to anyone before Daddy had even sailed it with you," she said. "You'll have to be specially good and helpful the next week or two, so that Daddy won't feel so disappointed in you."

Both the twins were miserable, and, to make things worse, Harry was angry because Terry didn't bring the ship back again.

"I can't," said Terry. "And I warn you, if I do, my father will come round and get it back—and you'll get some pretty hard things said to you. My father doesn't think much of you."

So Harry didn't dare to say much more. He was afraid of Terry's father! But he kept hinting that he was going to call in and see their mother.

"And I'll ask her how the kitten is getting on," he said. "Shall I?"

Snowy was getting on famously! It was a

beautiful little creature now. Its eyes were no longer blue, but as green as cucumbers, and very wide and bright. The only thing wrong with it was its back leg, which still dragged a little, though the kitten could run quite fast on the other three. It could jump too, and the twins laughed to see it pouncing after a cotton reel they had tied to a bit of string.

Nobody knew it lived in the shed. When Mummy took Baby out for a walk in her pram, the twins let the kitten out and it played on the grass like a mad thing. It drank quite a lot of milk now, and ate the bits of bread too that Tessie put to soak in the milk. Sometimes, for a treat, it had odd bits of fish or pudding that the children saved for it from their own plates.

"What shall we do when it gets any bigger?" said Terry. "We can't keep it shut up all the time!"

"Oh dear—I don't know," said Tessie, taking the kitten into her arms. "Look, Terry—there's a jackdaw down on the lawn again. I wonder if it's the one that flew off with Mummy's thimble the other day."

"Yes—that was annoying of it!" said Terry, watching the big jackdaw strutting about on the grass. "Did you see it take it?"

"Yes," said Tessie. "Mummy had been sewing out here in the summer-house, watching Baby nearby in her pram. She went indoors to answer the telephone and left me with Baby. And suddenly the jackdaw flew into the summer-house, perched on the wooden table there, and then flew off with Mummy's best silver thimble!"

"And Mummy says that it must have seen her best brooch winking in the sun on her dressing-table," said Terry, "because that suddenly disappeared too. Daddy says that jackdaws love to take bright things."

The big black jackdaw strutted about, prying under bushes, and pecking at a worm on the grass. And then, quite suddenly Snowy leapt out of Tessie's arms and raced over

"Chack-chack-chack!"

the lawn, its bad leg dragging a little as it ran!

The kitten was almost on the jackdaw before the big bird even saw it. With a loud "chack-chack-chack!" the jackdaw rose in the air, and flew away at once. The children laughed at the kitten's surprise.

"You'll have to get used to birds flying off into the air!" said Terry. "You brave little thing! The bird was much bigger than you!"

Snowy was very playful indeed. He grew more beautiful every day, and had a magnificent coat of soft, very white fur. He had learnt to wash himself now, and spent a long time keeping himself as white as snow. He knew his name and came running to the door of the shed, mewing loudly, as soon as he heard the twins coming, calling to him in a low voice.

His mew became so loud that the twins began to be afraid Mummy would hear him when she came into the garden to put Baby's pram out in the sun.

Terry felt worried. "I'm afraid that as I'm still in disgrace with Daddy, he'll be really *angry* if he finds out we've been keeping a kitten in secret," he said. "Then what will happen to Snowy?"

"He'll be sent away somewhere," said Tessie,

looking ready to cry. "And he'll be so unhappy because he loves us now."

Well, of course, a kitten can't be kept secret for ever, and a day came when Snowy was discovered! It happened very suddenly.

Mummy was sitting out on the lawn with Baby on a rug beside her, kicking merrily. Her next door neighbour, Mrs. Janes, called to her over the wall.

"How's that bonny baby of yours?"

Mummy left her deck-chair, and went over to the wall to have a little chat. And then, on big black wings, the jackdaw came flying down on the grass! It saw Baby Anne lying there kicking, and it caught sight of something shining brightly in her hand—her new silver rattle!

"Chack!" said the jackdaw, delighted to see the glittering thing, and it strutted up to the baby. It pecked at the silver rattle, but the baby wouldn't let go, staring at the black bird with big, frightened eyes. The jackdaw pecked again, and the baby yelled.

Mummy turned round at once, and saw the pecking jackdaw. She gave a scream—but before she could move towards the baby, someone else was there!

It pecked at the silver rattle

Snowy the kitten had seen the jackdaw from the window of his shed half-way down the garden. His sharp eyes watched the bird as it went over to the baby—and then, scrambling and pushing, the kitten forced open the little window and leapt down, landing with a bump that really surprised him. He got back his breath and raced on three legs over to the rug where the baby lay, with the jackdaw at the shining rattle.

Snowy leapt at the big bird—and with a frightened "chack-chack!" the jackdaw rose into the air, leaving one black feather in the kitten's mouth!

And then Mummy was there, picking up Baby Anne, and comforting her.

"There, there!" she said. "Naughty bird to

come and frighten Baby! And good gracious me—
WHERE did this brave little kitten come from? It
just scared the jackdaw away before it pecked *you*,
Baby!"

She sat down with Baby Anne on the rug, and
the kitten crept on to her skirt and lay there.
Mummy stroked it. "You dear, pretty little thing!
Whom do you belong to?"

At that moment the twins ran down the garden
to tell Mummy about the shopping they had just
been doing—and HOW surprised they were to see
Mummy petting the little white kitten! They stood
still in amazement.

"Look, darlings!" said Mummy. "Look at this
little pet of a kitten! That jackdaw came down and
saw Baby's shining silver rattle, and began to peck
at it, and frightened Baby—and this tiny thing
appeared from somewhere and drove the bird
away. I do wonder who it belongs to. Isn't it
sweet?"

"Yes—it's very sweet," said Tessie, not know-
ing what to say. "It's a darling."

"We must find out who the owner is," said
Mummy. "You can fetch the kitten a saucer of
milk—it really did save Baby from being badly
pecked. Dear me—how I wish it was *our* kitten! I

wouldn't mind having one like this, I really wouldn't!"

The twins could hardly believe their ears! "Mummy! Do you mean that?" said Terry at once. "Do you *really* wish it was ours?"

"Yes," said Mummy. "It's a most lovable little thing—look at it cuddling up to me. Do you know whose it is?"

"Yes," said Tessie. "Yes, we do know. It's *ours*, Mummy. Terry's and mine! Oh—please do say we can keep it!"

"AND NOW
IT'S REALLY OURS!"

WHEN Mummy heard Tessie say that
the kitten belonged to her and Terry,
she couldn't believe her ears. She
stared at the excited twins in astonishment.

"Now what exactly do you mean?" she said.
"The kitten *can't* be yours! I've never seen it before! Tell me all about it, please."

So, taking the kitten on to her knee, Tessie told
her mother how they had rescued the little thing
from drowning, and how they had gone to ask
Harry if he could help it, because his father was a
vet.

"And that's when I had to lend Harry my
ship," said Terry, "because he wouldn't help us
with the kitten unless I did! Miss Morgan, the
kennel-maid, told us how to look after it."

"We couldn't tell you because we knew you
didn't want a puppy or kitten till Baby could
walk," said Tessie. "But Mummy, it was such a
poor, poor little kitten, so wet and cold and thin
and hungry, we simply *had* to take it home."

"Darling Tessie," said Mummy, and put her

arm round the little girl. "I'm glad you did that. I'd have done it too! Poor little kitten—how could anyone be so cruel! And to think that, small as it was, it chased that big jackdaw away! Why, it might have pecked Baby very badly!"

"Mummy—do you really like the kitten then?" asked Terry, eagerly. "*Will* you keep it? It is growing big now and it was getting so difficult to hide it. You did say you wished it was ours, didn't you?"

"Yes, I did. And I meant it," said Mummy, stroking Snowy gently. "What a beautiful little creature it is! But we must do something about its leg. Perhaps Daddy will take it to the vet."

"Do you think Daddy will still feel disappointed in me, when he knows it was because of the kitten that I had to lend my new ship to Harry?" asked Terry, anxiously.

"He'll be *proud* of you, Terry, I promise you that!" said Mummy. "You're two good kind children, and *any* mother would be proud of you. We'll tell Daddy as soon as ever he comes home. Oh *look* at the kitten—it's cuddling up in my skirt again. It really *does* belong to us, doesn't it!"

The twins were very, very happy. Secrets were fun—but this one had become very worrying, especially after Daddy had found out about the ship being lent to Harry. It was lovely to feel that the kitten could be with them now whenever they wanted it.

"We'll be very careful not to let Snowy get under your feet, Mummy," said Tessie. "I'll put

"It really does belong to us"

him into my room whenever I know you've got to carry Baby anywhere."

"Oh, it seems such a sensible little thing, I'm sure it won't trip me up," said Mummy, who really did think Snowy was wonderful. "I'm longing to tell Daddy all about it."

Daddy was *most* astonished when he heard the story. He sat and listened as the twins and Mummy told him all about it, shaking his head in amazement.

"A kitten! And it's been here such a long time and we never guessed!" he said. "No wonder Mummy thought there were mice squeaking in the boxroom! Let me hold it—it looks a pet."

The kitten sniffed at Daddy's hands and then settled down on his knee, purring loudly.

"There! It knows it belongs to you too, Daddy," said Tessie, delighted. "Hark at it telling you!"

"I understand about the ship now, Terry," said Daddy, stroking Snowy. "And although I scolded you hard about it, I think it was kind of you to give up something you were proud of in order to get help for the kitten. I shall have a few words to say to Harry about that, though!"

"There's something wrong with its leg," said Mummy. "It drags that back one a bit, Daddy. We must have it seen to before it gets stiff for always."

"We'll take it straight round to the vet this very minute," said Daddy. "I'll telephone to him to say we're coming. Hold the kitten, Terry."

"Daddy—you're not disappointed in me any more, are you?" said Terry, anxious that everything should be absolutely right between him and his father now. It had worried him very much to feel that his father wasn't proud of him.

"Disappointed! I'm only sorry I didn't understand what was happening," said Daddy, clapping Terry on the back. "I wouldn't have scolded you at all, you know that. I'm prouder of you—and Tessie too—than I ever was before!"

Daddy, Terry and Tessie took the kitten round to the vet. He was kind and gentle, and examined the stiff little leg carefully.

"Leave it with me tonight," he said. "I shall have to manipulate it a little—I can put it right, but I may have to put the kitten to sleep while I do it. When it wakes up, its leg will hurt it a little —but it will be quite all right in a few days!"

"Oh, *thank* you!" said Tessie, delighted. "Isn't it a lovely kitten, Mr. Williams?"

"It's a beauty!" said the vet, stroking it. "I can't think how anyone could have been foolish enough, as well as unkind enough, to throw it into a pond—it's a kitten that could win a prize any day, when it grows up. I suppose they didn't want a kitten with a bad leg! Leave it with me now."

"Thank you," said the twins' father. "Now— may I have a word with your boy Harry, please? Where is he?"

"In the garden somewhere," said the vet. "Will you tell my next patient to come in please, as you go out? And don't worry about the kitten. It will be as right as rain tomorrow!"

They all went out. "Call Harry," said Daddy to Terry. "Look—there he is!"

Terry called loudly. "Harry! Harry, you're wanted!"

Harry came running up eagerly, hoping that he could perhaps get some more money out of Terry. He stopped very suddenly when he saw the twins' father.

"Come here, please, Harry," said Daddy. "I've  something to say to you. No—don't run away—unless you'd rather I said it to your father."

That made Harry come back at once, his face as red as a beetroot. He stood sulkily on the garden path.

"Take that scowl off your face," said

"Come here, Harry"

the twins' father. "You know what I want to say to you, don't you? I know all about your mean behaviour over the ship, and how you made Terry give you his money. I shall not tell your father this time—but NEXT time, there will be serious trouble. Do you understand?"

"I'll—I'll give back the fifty pence," mumbled Harry, very scared indeed. "Don't tell my father. He'll thrash me. I'll go and get the money now."

"You can give it to Terry tomorrow," said the twins' father. "He will be coming to fetch the kitten—and remember—any more of this kind of thing, and you'll find yourself really in trouble!"

They went out of the gate and left Harry shaking in his shoes. Goodness—to think that the twins' *father* knew all about his meanness! Harry made up his mind to turn over a new leaf at once, in case his *own* father got to hear of it!

It was a happy little family that went home that evening. The twins hung on to their father's arm, and told him every single thing about the kitten.

"And now it's to be *really* ours!" said Tessie, happily. "Oh, I do hope its leg will soon be better. Won't Baby love it when she's a bit bigger, Daddy?"

"Oh, we shall all love it!" said Daddy. "It looks as if Snowy will be the happiest kitten in the world. But how you managed to keep your secret so well, I really do not know!"

12. "ONE GOOD TURN DESERVES ANOTHER — PURR–PURR–PURR!"

NEXT morning the twins went to fetch the kitten from the vet's. Harry was at the gate, waiting for them. "Here's the money," he said, and pushed it into Terry's hand. "I'm sorry for what I did." And then away he went before they could say a word.

"Hallo, twins!" called Miss Morgan, the kennel-maid. "The vet's gone out to see to a horse that's had an accident. Here's your kitten—my word, hasn't it grown since you first brought it here! It's a beauty!"

"What about its leg?" asked Tessie, anxiously, stroking Snowy as he lay in the kennel-maid's arms.

"Quite all right," said Miss Morgan. "It will feel a bit bruised for a day or two—so don't be surprised if he still limps a little. But he will soon run on all four legs, and, if I know anything about it, he will be a regular little rascal!"

"Dear little Snowy!" said Tessie, and the kitten looked at her out of big green eyes, and purred loudly as she took it from Miss Morgan. "You're going to belong to the whole family now, instead of just to Terry and me."

"You know, this kitten must have come from quite a good litter of kittens," said Miss Morgan. "It's a real beauty. If I were you, I'd enter it for the Kitten Section of the Cat Show when it's held in a few weeks. It might win a prize for you."

"Really?" said Terry, in delight. "Do you hear that, Snowy? You might win a prize—how would you like that?"

The kitten mewed, and Miss Morgan laughed.

"It says it would like it very much, if it's something to eat!" she said. "Well good-bye now—I've about twelve pups to see to, and a few cats—a guinea-pig and some rabbits. I must go and see to my big family at once!"

In two days' time the kitten's leg was perfectly strong, and it could run on all fours, instead of only on three legs. Now that Mummy knew about it, it had the free run of the house, and was soon at home everywhere. Baby Anne loved it—and when Mummy put it on her pram for her to play with, it was as gentle as could be, and didn't put out one single claw. Mummy didn't fall over it once—even though it liked to hide under beds and chairs and leap out at any passing feet.

"It's really quite easy to watch out for it," said Mummy. "I was silly not to let you have one before. We might perhaps have a puppy next, while Snowy is still a kitten. Then they could grow up together!"

"For Christmas, Mummy!" said the twins, both together. "A black one, and we'll call it Sooty," added Terry. "Snowy and Sooty—that would be fun!"

One day Daddy took Terry down to the river to sail his ship—and how beautifully it sailed there, tugging at its string. All its rigging had been renewed, and the keel had been mended. Terry was very proud when he saw so many boys coming up to watch the *Flying Swan*.

On the way home Terry spotted a big notice in a shop.

"Look, Daddy!" he said. "The Cat Show is on next month, and there's a class for kittens. Miss Morgan said Snowy was a fine kitten and we ought to put him into the Cat Show. Can we? Do let's!"

"Well, of course," said Daddy. "I'll be very surprised if there's a prettier kitten than our Snowy! WHAT a good thing you were sailing your ship on the pond, when the poor little thing was thrown into the water!"

"Yes—and how surprised that person would be if he—or she—could see the kitten now!" said Terry. "Quick, let's get back home and tell Tessie about the Cat Show."

Tessie was very excited. She picked up Snowy and patted him. "We'll brush you, and give you a lovely green ribbon to match your eyes!" she said. "Do try and win a prize, Snowy, even if it's only a little one! We'd be prouder still of you then!"

By the time the Cat Show came, Snowy was the funniest, most mischievous kitten that any of them had ever seen. Daddy said he had never laughed so much in his life as he had since Snowy arrived in the family.

"He saw himself in the mirror yesterday," said Daddy, "and thought it was another cat there. So he tried to make friends with it, and purred loudly, and patted the glass. Then when the kitten in the mirror wouldn't make friends, he flew at it and tried to bite it—and couldn't think why he got his nose bumped so hard!"

On the day of the Show Tessie brushed Snowy till his coat gleamed like the snow itself. Then she tied a green ribbon round his neck to match his eyes.

"You look good enough to have your picture on a chocolate box!" she said. "Mummy, isn't he lovely? Do you think he will win a prize? We've entered him in the 'White Kitten' class and the 'Prettiest Kitten' class as well."

"He won't get a prize in the 'White Kitten' class," said Mummy, "because usually kittens belonging to Prize Pedigree Cats win those prizes. But he might win a Prettiest Kitten prize. You have certainly made him look very fine, Tessie!"

Very proudly the children carried Snowy to the Cat Show in a closed basket with a handle. They entered his name in the White Kitten Class and the Prettiest Kitten class too. He was put in a cage alongside many other cages of kittens—and, how strange, next to him was a white kitten almost EXACTLY like him! The man in charge of it stared at Snowy in surprise.

"Where did you get that kitten?" he said. "It might be the twin of mine!"

Terry told him. "Somebody threw it into the pond to drown it, and we rescued it. It had a bad leg, poor little thing, and we think that was why it was thrown away."

"A bad leg!" said the man, and turned and said something to the boy with him. Terry couldn't help hearing what he said. "Do you suppose that's the one we didn't want, because of the leg, Leonard? It's the living image of ours here—green eyes and all!"

"Sh!" said the boy, and frowned at the man. "They'll hear you!"

The twins *had* heard, of course, and they looked at one another in disgust. Was *this* the boy who had tried to drown their kitten?

Soon the judges came along—and they exclaimed in delight when they saw Snowy. And then they saw the white kitten in the next cage, so exactly like him. They examined them both carefully, and scribbled notes on their cards. Then they passed on.

And will you believe it, when the prize-winners' names were called out over the microphone, Snowy had won *both* the Kitten Prizes—first prize in the White Kitten class, and the first prize in the Prettiest Kitten one as well. The twins could hardly believe their ears!

"Did you hear that, Snowy?" said Tessie, putting her hand into the kitten's cage and stroking its soft fur. "You've won *two* prizes. You've beaten all the other kittens!"

The man and the boy who owned the kitten in

the next cage were angry, for they thought their
own kitten would easily win. They glared at
Snowy.

"Just because its eyes are greener than our
kitten's!" said the boy. "I wish I'd drowned it
properly."

"Well, it serves you right," said Tessie, unex-
pectedly, remembering again the tiny, wet,

"It—just—serves—you—RIGHT!"

frightened little thing that Terry had rescued from
the pond. "It—just—serves—you—RIGHT!"

"I don't know what you're talking about, you
silly little girl," said the man. But he did, of
course!

The twins carried Snowy home in triumph, and

the prizes too. Two whole pounds, one for each win—and cards to say that Snowy was the "Best White Kitten in Show" and the "Prettiest Kitten in Show" as well.

"We'll buy you a lovely basket of your own, with a cushion inside," said Tessie, joyfully. "Won't Mummy be pleased at the news!"

She was! She cuddled Snowy, and he patted her with his tiny paw. "You shall certainly have a new basket for your very own," she said, and the kitten mewed loudly, and purred.

"What did you say?" said Mummy. "Oh—you want Tessie to buy herself a pretty brooch—and Terry to buy a new railway signal for his electric train? Well, that's kind of you, Snowy. I'll give them back a pound of your prize money—here it is, twins!"

"But—do you suppose Snowy *really* wants us to do that?" said Tessie, pleased.

"Of course! He loves you, doesn't he?" said Mummy. "And I'm sure I know what he's purring to you this very minute. Listen! Can't you hear him purring, 'One good turn deserves another, one good turn deserves another, purr-purr-purr!'"

Snowy jumped on to Tessie's shoulder and purred in her ear, rubbing his head against her—

and then he jumped on to Terry's and did exactly
the same!

"He's telling us again!" said Tessie. "All right,
Snowy—we'll share your prize-money. Thank you
VERY much! Oh Mummy—don't you wish some-

Snowy jumped on to Tessie's shoulder

one could tell the story of our Birthday Kitten?
I do!"

Well—I've told it—and now there's nothing
more to say except a few words from Snowy himself. "Purr-rr-rr-rr-rr!"

The Boy
Who Wanted a Dog

by

Enid Blyton

Illustrated by David Dowland

RED FOX

CONTENTS

"HALLO, Granny!" said Donald, rushing in from afternoon school. "I hope you've come to tea!"

"Yes, I have!" said Granny. "And I've come to ask you a question, too. It's your birthday soon—what would you like me to give you?"

"He really doesn't deserve a birthday present," said his father, looking up from his paper. "His weekly reports from school haven't been good."

"Well, Dad—I'm not brainy like you," said Donald, going red. "I do try. I really do. But arithmetic beats me, I just *can't* do it. And I just hate trying to write essays and things—I can't seem to think of a thing to say!"

"You *can* work if you want to," said his mother, beginning to pour out the tea. "Look what your master said about your nature work—'Best work in the whole form. Knows more about birds and animals than anyone.' Well, why can't you do well at writing and arithmetic?"

"They're not as interesting as nature," said Donald. "Now, when we have lessons about dogs and horses and squirrels and birds, I don't miss a word! And I write jolly good essays about *them*!"

"Did you get good marks today?" asked his father.

Donald shook his head, and his father frowned. "I suppose you sat dreaming as usual!" he said.

"Well—geography was so dull this morning that I somehow couldn't keep my mind on it," said Donald. "It was all about things called peninsulas and isthmuses."

"And what *were* you keeping your mind on— if it happened to be working?" asked his father.

"Well—I was thinking about a horse I saw when I was going to school this morning," said Donald, honestly.

"But why think of a *horse* in your geography lesson?" said his mother.

"Well, Mother—it was a nice old horse, and doing its best to pull a heavy cart," said Donald. "And I couldn't help noticing that it had a dreadful sore place on its side, that was being rubbed by the harness. And oh, Mother, instead of being sorry for the horse, the man was hitting it!"

"And so you thought of the horse all through your geography lesson?" said Granny, gently.

"Well, I couldn't help it," said Donald. "I kept wondering if the man would put something on the sore place, when he got the horse home. I kept thinking what *I* would do if it were *my* horse. Granny, people who keep animals should be kind

"A puppy of my very own!"

to them, and notice when they are ill or hurt, shouldn't they?"

"Of course they should," said Granny. "Well, don't worry about the horse any more. I'm sure the man has tended it by now. Let's talk of something happier. What would you like for your birthday?"

"Oh Granny—there's something I want more

than anything else in the world!" said Donald, his eyes shining.

"Well, if it's not *too* expensive and is possible to get, you shall have it!" said Granny. "What is it?"

"A puppy!" said Donald, in an excited voice. "A puppy of my very own! I can make him a kennel myself. I'm good with my hands, you know!"

"*No*, Donald!" said his mother, at once. "I will *not* have a dirty little puppy messing about the house, chewing the mats to pieces, rushing about tripping everyone up, and . . ."

"He wouldn't! He wouldn't!" said Donald. "I'd train him well. He'd walk at my heels. He could sleep in my bedroom on a rug. He could . . ."

"Sleep in your room! Certainly not!" said his mother quite shocked. "No, Granny—*not* a puppy, please. Donald's bad enough already, the things he brings home—caterpillars, a hedgehog —ugh, the prickly thing—a stray cat that smelt dreadful and stole the fish out of the larder— and . . ."

"Oh Mother—I wouldn't bring *any*thing into the house if only you'd let me have a puppy!" said Donald. "It's the thing I want most in the world. A puppy of my very own! Granny, please, please give me one."

"NO," said his father. "You don't *deserve* a puppy while your school work is so bad. Sorry, Granny. You'll have to give him something else."

Granny looked sad. "Well, Donald—I'll give you some books about animals," she said. "Perhaps your father will let you have a puppy when you get a fine school report."

"I never will," said poor Donald. "I'm not nearly as clever as the other boys, except with my hands. I'm making you a little foot-stool, Granny, for *your* birthday. I'm carving a pattern all round it—and the woodwork master said that even *he* couldn't have done it better. I'm good with my hands."

"You've something else that is good too," said Granny. "You've a good heart, Donald, and a kind one. Well, if you mayn't have a puppy for your birthday, you must come with me to the bookshop and choose some really lovely books. Would you like one about dogs—and another about horses, or cats?"

"Yes. I'd like those very much," said Donald. "But oh—how I'd LOVE a puppy."

"Let's change the subject," said his father. "What about tea? I see Mother has made some of her chocolate cakes for you, Granny. Donald, forget this puppy business, please, and take a chair to the table for Granny."

So there they all are, sitting at the tea-table, eating jam sandwiches, chocolate buns and biscuits. Donald isn't talking very much. He is thinking hard—"dreaming", as his teacher would say.

"Where would I keep the puppy if I had one?" he thinks. "Let me see—I could make a dear little kennel, and put it in my own bit of garden. How pleased the puppy would be to see me each morning. What should I call him—Buster? Scamper? Wags? Barker? No—he mustn't bark, Mother would be cross. I'll teach him to . . ."

"Look! Donald's dreaming again!" said his mother. "Wake up, Donald! Pass Granny the buns! I wonder what you're dreaming about *now*!"

Granny knew! She smiled at him across the table. Dear Donald! WHY couldn't she give him the puppy that he so much wanted?

TWO days later Donald had quite an adventure! It was all because of a kitten. He was walking home from school, swinging his satchel, and saying "Hallo" to all the dogs he met, when he suddenly saw a kitten run out of a front gate. It was a very small one, quite black, fluffy and round-eyed.

"I'll have to take that kitten back into its house, or it will be run over!" thought Donald, and began to run. But someone else had seen it too—the dog across the road. Ha—a kitten to chase! What fun!

And across the road sped the dog, barking. The kitten was terrified, and tried to run up a nearby tree—but it wasn't in time to escape the dog, who stood with his fore-paws on the trunk of the tree, snapping at the kitten's tail and barking.

"Stop it! Get down!" shouted Donald, racing up. "Leave the kitten alone!"

The dog raced off. Donald looked at the terrified kitten, clinging to the tree-trunk. Was it hurt?

He picked it gently off the tree and looked at it. "You poor little thing—the dog has bitten your tail—it's bleeding. Whatever can I do? I'll just take you into the house nearby and see if you belong there."

But no—the woman there shook her head. "It's not *our* kitten. I don't know who it belongs to.

"Leave the kitten alone!"

It's been around for some time, and nobody really wants it. That's why it's so thin, poor mite."

"What a shame!" said Donald, stroking the frightened little thing. It cuddled closer to him, digging its tiny claws into his coat, holding on tightly. It gave a very small mew.

"Well—I'd better take it home," thought Donald. "I can't possibly leave it in the street.

That dog would kill it if he caught it! But whatever will Mother say? She doesn't like cats."

He tucked it gently under his coat and walked home, thinking hard. What about that old tumble-down shed at the bottom of the garden? He could put a box there with an old piece of cloth in it for the kitten—and somehow he could manage to make the door shut so that it would be safe.

"You see, your tail is badly bitten," he said to the kitten, whose head was now peeping out of his coat. "You can't go running about with such a hurt tail. I'll have to get some ointment and a bandage."

Donald thought he had better not take the kitten into the house. There might be a fuss. So he took the little thing straight to the old shed at the bottom of the garden. He saw an old sack there and put it into a box. Then he put the kitten there, and stroked it, talking in the special voice he kept for animals—low and kind and comforting. The kitten gave a little purr.

"Ah—so you can purr, you poor little thing! I shouldn't have thought there was a purr left in you, after your fright this morning!" said Donald. "Now I'm going to find some ointment and a bandage—and some milk perhaps!"

He shut the shed door carefully, and put a big

stone across the place where there was a hole at the bottom. Then he went down to the house. "Is that you, Donald?" called his mother. "Dinner will be ready in ten minutes."

Ten minutes! Good! There would be time to find what he wanted and go quickly back to the shed. He ran into the kitchen, which was empty—his mother was upstairs. Quickly he went to the cupboard where medicines and ointments were kept, and took out a small pot and a piece of lint.

Then he took an old saucer, went to the larder, and poured some milk into it. He tiptoed out of the kitchen door into the garden, thankful that no one had seen him.

Up to the old shed he went. The kitten was lying peacefully in the box, licking her bitten tail.

"I wouldn't use your rough little tongue on that sore place," said Donald. "Let me put some ointment on it. It will feel better then. Perhaps it's a good thing, really, you've licked it—it's your way of washing the hurt place clean, I suppose. Now, keep still—I won't hurt you!"

And, very gently, he took the kitten on to his knee and stroked it. It began to purr. Donald dipped his finger into the ointment and rubbed it gently over the bitten place. The kitten gave a sudden yowl of pain and almost leapt off his knee!

"Sorry!" said Donald, stroking it. "Now keep still while I wrap this bit of lint round your tail, and tie it in place."

The kitten liked Donald's soft, gentle voice. It lay still once more, and let the boy put on the piece of lint—but when he tied it in place, it yowled again, and this time managed to jump right off his knee to the ground!

Donald had put the saucer of milk down on the floor when he had come to the shed, and the kitten suddenly saw it. It ran to it in surprise, and began to lap eagerly, forgetting all about its hurt tail.

The boy was delighted. He had bound up the bitten tail, and had given the kitten milk—the two things he had come to do. He bent down and stroked the soft little head.

"Now you keep quiet here, in your box," he said. "I'll come and see you as often as I can."

He opened the door while the kitten was still lapping its milk, shut it, and went up the garden. He was happy. He liked thinking about the tiny creature down in the shed. It was his now. It was a shame that nobody had wanted it or cared for it. What a pity his mother didn't like cats! If she had loved it, it could have had such a nice home.

"I'll have to find a home for it," he thought.

"I'll get its tail better first, and then see if I can find someone who would like to have it!"

The kitten drank a little more milk, climbed back into its box, sniffed at the lint round its tail, and went sound asleep. Sleep well, little thing— you are safe for the night!

IT WAS not until the next morning that Donald found a chance to slip down to the shed to see the kitten. He took some more milk with him, and a few scraps.

"It will be so hungry!" he thought. "What a good thing I left it some milk!"

But the milk had hardly been touched, and the kitten was lying very still in its box. It gave a faint mew when Donald bent over it, as if to say, "Here's that kind boy again!"

"You don't look well, little kitten," said Donald, surprised. "What's the matter? You haven't lapped up the milk I left!"

He knew what the matter was when he saw the kitten's tail. It was very swollen, and the tiny creature had torn off the bandage with its teeth! It was in pain, and looked up at the boy as if to say "*Please* help me!"

"Oh dear—something has gone wrong with your poor little tail!" said Donald. "Perhaps the wound has gone bad, like my finger did when I gashed it on a tin. *Now* what am I to do with you?"

The kitten lay quite still, looking up at Donald. "I can't take you indoors," said the boy. "My mother doesn't like cats. I think I'd better take you to the vet. You needn't be frightened. He's an animal doctor, and he loves little things like you. He'll make your tail better, really he will!"

"Mew-ew!" said the kitten, faintly, glad to see this boy with the kind voice and gentle hands. It cried out when he lifted it up and put it under his coat.

"Did I hurt your poor tail?" said Donald. "I couldn't help it. If we go quickly I'll have time to take you to the vet's as soon as he's there. It's a good thing it's Saturday, else I would have had to go to school."

There were already three people in the vet's surgery when Donald arrived—a man with a dog, whose paw was bandaged; a woman with a parrot that had a drooping wing—and a small girl with a pet mouse in a box. One by one they were called into the surgery—and at last it was Donald's turn.

The vet was a big man with big hands—hands that were amazingly gentle and deft. He saw at once that the kitten's tail was in a very bad state.

"It was bitten by a dog," said Donald. "I did my best—put ointment on and bound it up."

"You did well," said the vet. "Poor mite! I'm afraid it must lose half its tail. It's been bitten too badly to save. But I don't expect it will worry overmuch at having a short tail!"

"Perhaps the other cats will think it's a Manx cat," said Donald. "Manx cats have short tails, haven't they?"

"It was bitten by a dog."

The vet smiled. "Yes. Now you'll have to leave the kitten with me, and I must deal with its tail. It will be quite all right. It won't be unhappy here."

Donald liked the vet very much. His big hands held the kitten very gently, and the little thing began to purr.

"Do all animals like you, sir?" he asked.

"Oh yes—animals always know those who are their friends," he said. "That kitten knows *you* are its friend. It will let you handle it without fear. I'll keep it for a week, then you can have it back."

"Er—how much will your bill be?" asked Donald.

"Oh, *you* needn't worry about that!" said the vet. "I'll send the bill in to your father."

"But, sir—my father and mother don't know about the kitten," said Donald. "You see—I kept it in my shed. It isn't mine, it's a stray. My mother doesn't like animals very much—especially cats. I'd like to pay your bill myself, sir. The only thing is—I haven't much money just at present."

"Well, now, would you like to earn a little, by helping me?" said the vet. "You could pay off the bill that way! My kennel-maid is away for a few days—she looks after the dogs here for me—feeds them and brushes them. *You* could do that, couldn't you, for a few evenings?"

"Oh YES! Yes, I could," said Donald, really delighted. "I'd *love* to. But would you trust me to do the job properly, sir? We've never had a dog at home. But I love dogs, I really do."

"I'd trust any boy with any animal here, if he handled a kitten as gently as you do," said the vet. "It isn't everyone who has the gift of understanding animals, you know. You're lucky!"

"My Granny says that anyone who loves animals understands them," said Donald.

"She's right," said the vet. "Now look—I've more patients waiting for me, as you saw. Leave the kitten in that basket. I'll attend to it as soon as I can. Come back tonight at half-past five, and I'll introduce you to the dogs. Right?"

"Yes, sir," said Donald, joyfully, and put the kitten gently into the basket on the floor. Then out he went, very happy.

The kitten would be all right now. He could pay the bill by taking the job the vet offered him—and what a job! Seeing to dogs—feeding them—perhaps taking them for walks! But wait a bit—what would his parents say?

He told his father first. "Daddy, the vet wants a boy to help him a bit while his kennel-maid is away," said Donald. "I thought I'd take the job —it's in the evenings—and earn a bit of money. You're always saying that boys are lazy nowadays—not like when you were young, and went out and earned money even while you were at school."

"Well! I didn't think you had it in you to take a job like that!" said his father. "I'm pleased. So long as you don't neglect your homework, you can help the vet. Well, well—and I thought you were such a lazy young monkey!"

Donald was delighted. He could hardly wait for the evening to come! Looking after dogs! Would they like him? Would he be able to manage them? Well—he would soon know!

DONALD could hardly wait for the evening to come. He did his usual Saturday jobs—ran errands for his mother, cleaned his father's bicycle and his own, and weeded a corner of the garden.

Then his mother called him. "What's this I hear from your father about your working for the vet? You know he's an *animal* doctor? You'll come home all smelly and dirty!"

"I shan't, Mother," said Donald, in alarm. "Goodness me, you should see the vet's place—as clean as our own! Anyway, Dad says it will be good for me."

"Well, if you *do* come home smelling of those animals up at the vet's place, you'll have to give up the job," said his mother. "Fancy *wanting* to go and work with animals! I'm surprised at your father letting you!"

Donald kept out of his mother's way all day, really afraid that she would forbid him to go up to the vet's house that evening. He put on his very oldest clothes, and, when at last the clock said a quarter-past-five, off he went at top speed on his bicycle. His first job! And with dogs too! how lucky he was!

He arrived at the vet's, put his bicycle in a shed and went to find the kennels. The vet was there, attending to a dog with a crushed paw.

"Ah—you're here already, Donald!" he said. "Good—you're early, so you can give me a hand with this poor old fellow. He's had such a shock that he's scared stiff. I want to calm him down before I do anything."

"What happened?" asked Donald, shocked to see the poor, mis-shapen front paw of the trembling dog.

"It was caught in a door," said the vet. "Apparently the wind slammed the door shut, and he couldn't get his paw away in time. He's a nervy dog. Do you think you can hold him still while I examine the paw?"

"I don't know. I'll try," said Donald. He stroked the dog and spoke to it in his "special" voice—the one he used for animals. "Poor old boy—never mind—you'll soon be able to walk on that paw. Poor old boy, then, poor old boy."

The dog turned to him, pricked its ears, and listened. Then it licked Donald on the cheek, and gave a little whine of pain.

"Go on talking to him," said the vet. "Don't stop. He's listening to you. He won't mind about me if you take his attention."

So Donald went on talking and stroking, and

the dog listened, trying to get as close to the boy as he could. This boy was a comforting boy. This

"Well, that's it," said the vet.

boy had a lovely, clean, boy-smell. He was worth listening to!

The dog gave a little whine now and again as the vet worked on his hurt paw. Soon the vet spoke to him. "Nearly over now, old dog. I'm putting a plaster on, so don't be afraid. You'll be able to walk all right, your foot will be protected. Nearly over now."

The dog gave a huge sigh and laid his head on Donald's shoulder. Donald was so happy to feel it there that he could hardly speak to the dog for a moment. He found himself repeating what the vet had said. "Nearly over now, old dog, nearly over now."

"Well—that's it," said the vet, standing up. "Come on, old dog—to your kennel, now, and a nice long sleep."

The dog followed him, limping. Donald went too. The dog licked his hand every now and again, as if thanking him. The vet put him into a roomy kennel with straw on the floor, and shut the door. "Goodnight, old dog!" called Donald, and from the kennel came a short bark—woof-woof!

"He'll be all right," said the vet. "You did well to hold him, youngster—a big dog like that. You have a good voice for animals, too. Now, here are the dogs I want you to brush, and to give fresh water to. Clean up any kennels that need it. You'll find fresh straw yonder if necessary."

Donald had never had such an interesting evening in all his life. There were five dogs in the kennels, each in a separate one—and all the dogs were different! He looked at them carefully.

"An alsatian—a labrador—goodness, he's fat—and a corgi with stubby little legs. He looks very intelligent. What's this dog, over in the kennel corner—a little black poodle—what a pet! And this last one—well, goodness knows what it is—a real mixture. A bit of a terrier, a bit of a spaniel, and a bit of something else!"

The dogs barked with joy when the boy came to them. They loved company of any sort and were longing for a walk.

"Three of them are here because their owners are away from home," said the vet. "The corgi has a bad ear. The little mongrel ate something he shouldn't and nearly poisoned himself, but he's feeling better now. You won't be scared of going into their kennels, will you? Their bark is worse than their bite!"

"Oh *no*, sir, I'm not scared!" said Donald. "Shall I take them for a walk when I've finished?"

"Not tonight—we're a bit late," said the vet. "I'll take them out myself, last thing. You get on with the brushing."

He left Donald alone. The boy was too happy for words. He had five dogs to see to—five! And what was more, they all seemed as pleased to see him, as he was to see them!

"Hallo, all of you!" he said. "I'm just going to fetch a can of fresh water for you. Then I'll clean out your kennels, put down fresh straw, and have a word with each of you. Shan't be long."

And off he went, whistling loudly, to the tap he saw in the distance. He filled a large can with water, and went back to the dogs. They were whining and barking now, the bigger ones standing with their paws on the top of their gates.

"I like you all very much," said Donald, in his "special" voice. "I hope you like me too."

"Woof-woof, WUFF, whine-whine, WOOF-WOOF!" Yes, they certainly liked Donald, no doubt about that. WOOF!

DONALD had a wonderful evening with the five dogs. He went first into the labrador's kennel—it was rather like a small shed with a half-door or gate at the front, to get in by, fastened with a latch on the outer side.

The labrador was a big dog, a lovely golden colour. He stared at Donald in silence as the boy went in. "Hallo!" said Donald. "How are you? Sorry I don't know your name. I've brought you some fresh water, and I'll sweep out your kennel and give you some fresh straw. Will you like that?"

The labrador lumbered over to the boy and sniffed his legs and hands. Then he wagged his tail slowly. Donald patted him. "Are you homesick?" he said. "Poor old boy! Do you miss your master?"

At the word "master" the labrador pricked up his ears and gave a little whine. Donald emptied out the water-bowl, wiped it round with a cloth he had found by the tap, and poured in fresh water. The labrador lapped it eagerly. He didn't like stale water—this was lovely and cold and fresh! He sniffed at Donald again, decided that he liked him, and licked his bare knee.

Donald patted him, delighted. "Sorry I can't stay long with you," he said. "I've the other dogs

"You must be a thirsty dog!"

to see to. But I'll be back to give you a brush-down when I've finished."

He went to the alsatian's kennel next. This too was a big one, almost a shed. "Hallo!" said Donald. "My word, you've a big water-bowl— you must be a thirsty dog! Hey, don't drink out of the can, Greedy! That's right—you've plenty

in your bowl! I'll come back again soon and brush
you."

The alsatian stopped drinking and went to his
gate with Donald, hoping to get out and have a
run. "No, old boy," said Donald, firmly. "You'll
have to wait for your walk till the vet takes you
out tonight. Hey, let me get out of the gate!"

He went to the poodle next, a dear little woolly-
coated thing that danced about on tiptoe as soon
as the boy came into her kennel. She licked
Donald everywhere she could.

"I shall have to bring a towel with me when I
come to see *you*," said Donald. "You really have
a VERY wet tongue. Now—drink your water. I'll
be back again in a minute!"

The other two dogs, the corgi and the mongrel,
were not feeding very well, especially the corgi,
whose ear was hurting him. They wagged their
tails and whined when Donald went in to them.
The mongrel was very thirsty and drank all his
water at once. Donald patted him.

"You're thin," he said. "And you look sad.
I'll bring you some more water when I come in
to clean your kennel."

The mongrel pressed himself against the boy's
legs, grateful for attention and kindness. He
whined when Donald went out. That was a nice
boy, he thought. He wished he could spend the

night with him. He would cuddle up to him and perhaps he would feel better then!

The next thing was to clean out the kennels, and put in fresh straw. Once more the dogs were delighted when Donald appeared, and gave him loud and welcoming barks.

The vet, at work in his surgery, looked out of the window, pleased. The dogs sounded happy. That boy had made friends with them already. Ah, there he was, carrying a bundle of straw!

Donald cleaned out each kennel and put down fresh straw—and the five dogs nuzzled him and whined lovingly while he was in their kennels. He talked to them all the time, and they loved that. They listened with ears pricked, and gave little wuffs in answer. They gambolled round him, and licked his hand whenever they could. Donald had never felt so happy in all his life.

He had to brush down each dog after he had cleaned the kennels, and this was the nicest job of all. The dogs really loved feeling the firm brushing with the hard-bristled brush. Each dog had his own brush, with his name on it, so to the dogs' delight, Donald suddenly knew their names, and called them by them!

When he had finished his evening's work, he patted each dog and said goodnight. All five dogs stood up with their feet on their gates, watching him go, giving little barks as if to say, "Come back tomorrow! Do come back!"

"I'll be back!" called Donald, and went up to

It mewed with delight when it saw Donald.

the surgery to report that he had finished. The vet clapped him on the shoulder and smiled.

"I've never heard the dogs so happy. Well

done. Tomorrow is Sunday. Will you be able to come?"

"Oh yes—not in the morning, but I could come in the afternoon and evening, if you've enough jobs for me, sir!" said Donald. "I'll be glad to earn enough money to pay off the bill for the kitten! Could I see the kitten, sir? Is its tail better?"

"Getting on nicely," said the vet. "I've got it in the next room. Come and see it."

So into the next room they went, and there, in a neat little cage, lying on a warm rug, was the kitten. It mewed with delight when it saw Donald, and stood up, pressing its nose against the cage.

"It only has half a tail now," said the boy sadly. "Poor little thing. Is it in pain still?"

"Oh no—hardly at all," said the vet. "But I must keep it quiet until the wound has healed."

"What will happen to it?" asked Donald. "Nobody will want a kitten with only half a tail, will they? I *wish* my mother would let me keep it."

"Don't worry about that," said the vet. "We'll find a kind home for it. You've done a good evening's work. Come along tomorrow, and you can take the dogs for a walk. I really think I can trust you with the whole lot!"

Donald sped home in delight. As soon as he arrived there, he rushed upstairs, ran a bath for himself, and then put on clean clothes. "Now Mother won't smell a doggy smell at all!" he thought. "I just smell of nice clean soap! But oh, *I* think a doggy smell is lovely! I can't wait till tomorrow, I really can't!"

DONALD was very hungry for his supper. He had really worked hard that evening. His mother was surprised to see the amount of bread-and-butter that he ate with his boiled egg.

"What's made you so hungry?" she asked. "Oh, of course—you've been helping the vet, haven't you? What did you do?"

"I cleaned out the dog kennels—five of them," said Donald. "And I . . ."

"Cleaned out dog kennels! Whatever next?" said his mother, quite horrified.

"Well, I emptied the water-bowls and put in fresh water—and I brushed-down an alsatian called Prince, a labrador, a corgi, a poodle and a mongrel!" said Donald. "May I have some more bread-and-butter, please?"

His father began to laugh. "Boil him another egg, bless him," he said. "He's worked harder at the vet's this evening than he ever does at school. It's something to know that he can work well, even if it's just with dogs, and not with books."

"Well, these dogs are jolly interesting!" said Donald. "Dad, you should have seen how they all came round me—as if they'd known me for years!"

"That's all very well," said his mother, "but I do hope you won't forget your weekend homework in your excitement over these dogs."

"Gracious! Homework! Oh blow it—I'd forgotten all about it!" said Donald, in dismay. "It's those awful decimal sums again. I wish I could do sums about *dogs*—I'd soon do those! And I've an essay to write about some island or other—dull as ditch-water. Now, an essay about *dogs*—I could write pages!"

"Just forget about dogs for a bit and finish your supper," said his mother. "Then you really must do a little homework."

"I'm tired now. I'd get all my sums wrong," said Donald, yawning. "I'll do it tomorrow morning, before we go to church. I'm going to the vet's again in the afternoon and evening."

"My word—you *are* keen on your new job!" said his father. "I'm pleased about that. But I shall stop you going if your school-work suffers, remember."

Poor Donald! He really was tired that evening after his work with the dogs. He couldn't do his sums properly. His head nodded forward and he fell asleep. It was a good thing that his parents had gone out! When he awoke it was almost nine o'clock! He hastily put away his undone work and rushed up to bed, afraid that his parents would come in and find his homework still not done.

"I'll have time in the morning!" he thought. "I'll set my alarm clock and wake early. My mind is nice and clear then!"

So, when his alarm went at seven, he leapt out of bed, and tackled his sums. Yes—they *were* easier to do first thing in the morning. But oh that essay! He'd do that after breakfast. But after breakfast his mother wanted him to do some jobs for her—and then he had to get ready to go to church. That silly essay! What was the sense of writing about something he wasn't at all interested in? If only he could write about those five dogs! Goodness, he would be able to fill pages and pages!

He had told the vet that he would be at the surgery at half-past two. That left him just twenty minutes after midday dinner to do the essay! He took his pen and wrote at top speed, so that his writing was bad and his spelling poor, for he had no time to look up any words in the dictionary.

He looked at the rather smudgy pages when he had finished. His teacher would NOT be pleased. Oh dear—he really hadn't time to do it all over again. Maybe he could wake up early next morning and rewrite it!

Donald changed quickly into his old clothes and rushed out to get his bicycle. Then away he went, pedalling fast, glad that no one had stopped him, and asked him to do a job of some sort!

The boy had a wonderful afternoon. The vet took him into an airy little building where he kept birds that had been hurt, or were ill—and budgerigars that he bred himself for sale. Donald was enchanted with the gay little budgies. The vet let them out of their great cage, and they flew gaily round Donald's head, came to rest on his shoulder or his hand—and one even sat on his ear!

"Oh, how I'd love to breed budgies like these!" he said. "How I'd like a pair for my own!"

"Good afternoon," said a voice, suddenly, almost in Donald's ear. "How are you, how are you, how are you?"

Donald looked round in surprise—and then he laughed. "Oh—it's that parrot talking!" he said. "A lovely white parrot! Is he hurt, or something?"

"No. I'm just keeping him for a time because his owner is ill," said the vet. "He's a wonderful talker!"

"Shut the door! DO shut the door!" said the

parrot, and Donald obediently went to the door! The vet laughed.

"Don't shut it! It's just something he knows

Donald looked round in surprise.

how to say—one of the scores of things he's always repeating!"

The parrot cleared its throat exactly like Donald's father did. Then it spoke again, in a very cross voice. "Sit down! Stand up! Go to bed!"

Donald began to laugh—and the parrot

laughed too—such a human laugh that the boy was really astonished. Then the vet took him to a shed, where he kept any cats that needed his help. The little kitten was there too, curled up asleep, its short tail still bandaged. It looked very happy and contented. There were four big cats there also, one with a bandaged head, one with a leg in plaster.

"All my patients," said the vet, fondling one of them. "Cats are more difficult to treat than dogs—not so trusting. Mind that one—she's in pain at the moment, and might scratch you!"

But before the vet had even finished his sentence, Donald was stroking the cat, and talking to it in his "special" voice. It began to purr loudly, and put down its head for him to scratch its neck.

The vet was amazed. "Why, that cat will hardly let even *me* touch it!" he said. "Look, I have to change its bandage now—see if you can hold the cat quiet for me, will you? It fought me like a little fury this morning. Will you risk it? You may be well and truly scratched!"

"I'll risk it," said Donald, happily. "I love cats and kittens. Show me what to do, sir—how to hold her. Hark at her purring! *She* won't scratch me!"

"Be careful, Donald. Cats are different from dogs. If you go home with your face scratched and torn, you won't be allowed to go and help the vet again. So do be careful."

"WHAT'S the matter with the cat, sir?" asked Donald, as he went on fondling the nervous animal.

"Its hind legs somehow got caught in a trap," said the vet. "One has mended well, but the other is badly torn, and won't heal. So I have to paint the leg with some lotion that stings—and this the cat can't bear!"

"How did you manage to hold the cat, and deal with its leg at the same time?" asked Donald, as the cat began to stiffen itself in fright. "Did the kennel-maid hold it for you when she was here?"

"Oh no—she was frightened of the cat," said the vet. "It's half-wild, anyhow—lives in the woods. The keeper brought it to me. It's a lovely cat, really—half Persian. Now—can you hold it. I'll show you how to."

Gently the vet took the cat and showed the boy how to hold it for him. The cat suddenly spat at him and tried to leap away, her claws out. But the vet's hold was firm and kind.

"I see, sir. I see exactly." said Donald. "Poor old puss, then. Don't be scared. We're your friends, you know. Poor old Puss."

"Go on talking to the cat," said the vet. "It's

listening to you just like that hurt dog did. You've a wonderful voice for animals. Many children have, if only they knew it—it's a low, kind, soothing voice that goes on and on and animals can't *help* listening. Go on talking to the cat, Donald. It's quieter already."

The cat struggled a little as Donald held her, talking smoothly and quietly in his "animal" voice. Soon she lay limp in his hold, and let the vet do what he pleased with her bad leg. She gave a loud yowl once when the lotion suddenly stung, but that was all.

Soon the bandage was on again, and the cat lay quietly in Donald's arms, purring. "Shall I hold her for a bit, sir?" said the boy. "She sort of wants comforting, I think."

The vet looked at the boy holding the wounded cat. "You know, son, you should be a vet yourself when you grow up!" he said. "You could do anything with animals! They trust you. How'd you like to be an animal-doctor?"

"I'd like it more than anything in the world!" said Donald. "I love animals so much—and they love me, sir! They do, really. I've never had a real pet of my own—my parents aren't fond of animals—so I've always had to make do with caterpillars and a hedgehog or two, and once a little wild mouse . . ."

"And I don't suppose you were allowed to bring them into the house, were you?" said the vet. "Well, some people like animals and everything to do with nature—and some don't. We're the lucky ones, you and I, aren't we?"

"Yes. We are," said Donald, carrying the cat back to its cage. "It's not much good my thinking of being an animal-doctor, though, sir. I think I've got to go into my father's business and be an architect. And the awful thing is, I'm no good at figures or drawing or any of the things that architects have to do. I shall be a very very bad architect and hate every minute. And I shall keep dozens of stray animals in my backyard, just to make up for it!"

The vet laughed. "If you want a thing badly enough, you'll get it," he said. "You'll be a vet one day, and be as happy as the day is long! Now to work again!"

Donald spent a very happy Sunday at the vet's. He helped him with more of the animals, he cleaned out the birds' cages, and, best of all, he took all the five dogs for a long long walk!

The vet telephoned his parents to ask them if Donald could stay to tea with him, so he didn't need to rush home at half-past four. He went to fetch the dogs, calling "Who's for a walk, a WALK, a WALK!" They all began to bark in delight, and the alsatian did his best to jump right over the top of his high kennel-gate!

"Take them on the hills," said the vet. "There will be few people there, and you can let them loose for a good run. Whistle them when you want them to come to you. *Can* you whistle, by the way?"

Donald promptly whistled so long, loudly and clearly, that the vet jumped—and all the dogs in the kennels began to bark in excitement!

"Watch out for the corgi when you're on the hills," said the vet. "He may not be able to keep up with the others, on his short legs. And don't lose the mongrel down a rabbit-hole—he's a terror for rabbits!"

Donald set off happily, with the five dogs gambolling round him. They might have known him for years! Once on the hills they galloped about in joy. The mongrel promptly went half-way down a rabbit-hole, and Donald had to pull him out!

A man came walking down the hill towards them. Prince, the alsatian, immediately went to sniff at him, and the man shouted at him "Get away!" and struck out with his stick. The big alsatian growled at once, showing all his fine white teeth.

"Call your dog off!" yelled the angry man to

Donald—and the boy suddenly stopped in astonishment. Goodness—it was Mr. Fairly, his school-
teacher. He whistled to the alsatian, and the dog
returned to him at once—and so did the other

"Call your dog off!" yelled the angry man.

four! They all ran to him at top speed, and milled
round him in delight, whining for a pat.

Mr. Fairly was astounded to see Donald—the
dunce of the maths class—with five gambolling
dogs! "What in the world are you doing with this
army of dogs!" he yelled. "That alsatian's dangerous!"

"He's all right, sir!" yelled back Donald, quite pleased to have seen his fierce maths master scared of a dog. "I'm taking them all for a walk. Heel, boys, heel!"

And, to the master's astonishment, every dog obediently rushed to Donald's heels, and walked behind as meekly as school children. Well, well—the boy might not be able to do sums—but he could manage dogs all right! What a very surprising thing! There must be more in that boy than he had ever imagined!

I N THE week, Donald could only manage to go to the vet's in the evenings—and how he looked forward to the time after tea when he could slip off to the kennels and see to the dogs. They welcomed him with barks that could surely be heard half a mile away!

But poor Donald had a shock when Wednesday arrived, and the essays of the weekend came up for correction. He had handed in his smudgy, hastily written one, ashamed of it, but not having had enough time to do it again.

Mr. Fairly his form master had the piles of essays in front of him, and dealt with the good ones first, awarding marks. Then he looked sternly at Donald, and waved an exercise book at him—Donald's own book!

"This essay must be written all over again!" he said. "In fact, I'm almost inclined to say it should be written out *three* times. The spelling! The handwriting! The smudges! Donald, you should be in the lowest form, not this one! I am really ashamed to have a boy like you in my class."

"I'm sorry, sir. I—well—I had rather a lot to do in the weekend," said poor Donald.

"Ha yes—taking out dogs for a walk on the

hills, I suppose!" said Mr. Fairly. "Well, I shall ask your parents if they will please see that your homework is done—and done well—before you go racing off with the most peculiar collection of dogs that I have ever seen!"

"Oh please, sir, don't complain to my parents!" said Donald. "I'll re-write the essay, sir. I'll—I'll write it out *three* times if you like!"

"Very well. Rewrite your essay three times to-night, and hand it in tomorrow," said Mr Fairly. "I fear, Donald, that that will mean five dogs will have to do without your company after tea!"

"The mean fellow!" thought Donald, angrily. "He must *know* I am taking the vet's dogs walking after tea—and that's about the worst punishment he could give me—making me sit indoors, writing essays, when he knows I love walking the dogs!"

But there was nothing to be done about it—Donald had to tell the vet he wouldn't be up after tea that day.

"Bad luck," said the vet, kindly. "The dogs will miss you. Never mind. Just come when you can. I'll manage."

Donald sat down after tea to rewrite his essay. Blow, bother, blow! What a waste of a lovely evening! Would the dogs miss him? Would they be looking out for him? What a pity he couldn't write about *them*, instead of rewriting his stupid essay!

His mother was astonished to find him in his bedroom, writing so busily. "I thought you would be up at the vet's," she said. "Are you doing extra homework, or something?"

"Well—sort of," said Donald. His mother looked closely at what he was doing, and frowned.

"Oh Donald! You're rewriting an essay! And no wonder! WHAT a mess you made of it—however could you give in work like that? I suppose you wrote it in a hurry because you give up so much time to helping the vet."

"The weekend was so busy," said Donald, desperately. "I just had to hurry over my essay."

"Well, you know what Daddy said—you can only go to help the vet if your school-work is good," said his mother. "I'm afraid you mustn't go any more."

Donald stared at his mother, his heart going down into his boots. Not go any more? Not see those lovely dogs—and help with the cats and the birds? Not be with the vet again, the man he admired so much?

"I MUST go to the vet's," he said. "He's going to pay me for my work. I want the money for something."

"What for?" asked his mother, astonished.

Donald looked away. How could he tell her that he had taken that little kitten to the vet's to be healed and looked after, so that he might perhaps have it for his own pet, hidden away somewhere? How could he tell her that what he earned at the vet's was to pay for the kitten's treatment? She didn't like cats. So how could she understand what he felt for the tiny kitten that had been chased and bitten by a dog?

But it was all no good. His mother told his father about his badly written essay, and he agreed that if Donald's work was poor because he hadn't enough time for it, then of course he must give up helping the vet. And what was more, he telephoned the vet himself, and told him that Donald was not coming any more.

The vet was very sorry. He liked Donald—he liked the way he did his work with the animals—he would miss him. And what about that little kitten? Well—he must find a good home for it. A pity that boy had no pets of his own—he was marvellous with animals!

Donald was very unhappy. He missed going to the vet's. He missed the companionship of all the animals, so friendly and lively. He began to sleep badly at nights.

One night he lay awake for hours, thinking of the five dogs, the cats—and the little kitten with the half-tail. He wouldn't be able to see the kitten any more—and he somehow couldn't help feeling that it ought to belong to *him*.

He sat up in bed, and looked out towards the hill where the vet lived. "I've a good mind to dress and go up to the kennels," he thought. "The dogs will know me—they won't bark. They'll be very glad to see me. *They* don't mind if I'm no good at sums or essays. I'm quite good enough for *them*. They think I'm wonderful. I'm not, of course—but it *is* so nice to be thought wonderful by *some*body!"

He dressed quickly, and slipped quietly down the stairs. He let himself out by the back-door, locking it after him, and taking the key in case any burglar should try to get in.

"Now for the dogs!" he thought, feeling his heart lighter already. "They'll be so surprised and pleased! I'll feel better after I've been with them for a little while. Oh dear—sometimes I think that dogs are nicer than people!"

DONALD wheeled his bicycle quietly out of the shed, and was soon speeding along the dark roads, and up the hill to where the vet lived. "I'll just have half-an-hour with the dogs," he thought. "I'll feel much better when I've had a word with them, and felt their tongues licking me lovingly."

He was soon at the familiar gate, and rode in quietly. He put his bicycle into an empty shed, and went towards the kennels. Would the dogs bark, and give the alarm, telling the vet that someone was about in the night? Or would they know his footsteps, and keep quiet?

The dogs were asleep—but every one of them awoke almost as soon as Donald rode into the drive! Prince, the big alsatian, growled—and then, stopped, his ears pricked up. A familiar smell came on the wind to him—a nice, clean boy-smell—the smell of that boy who looked after him a week or so ago! The alsatian gave a little whine of joy.

The corgi was wide awake too, listening. He didn't growl. He felt sure it was the kind boy he liked so much. He tried to peer under his gate, but all he could see was the grass outside. Then he heard Donald's voice, and his tail at once began to wag.

Soon Donald was peering over the gates of the dogs' kennels. The alsatian went nearly mad with joy, but gave only a small bark of welcome, for Donald shushed him as soon as he saw him.

"Sh! Don't bark! You'll wake the vet. I'll come into each of your kennels and talk to you. I've missed you so!"

He went first into the alsatian's kennel, and the dog almost knocked him over, in his joy at seeing him. He could not help giving a few small barks of delight. He licked the boy all over, and pawed him, and rubbed his head against him. Donald stroked and patted, and even hugged him.

"It's so lovely to be with you again," he said. "I've missed you all so. I'm in disgrace, but *you* don't mind, do you? Now, calm down a bit—I'm going to see the other dogs. I'll come and say goodbye to you before I go!"

He left the alsatian's kennel and went to the next one. The corgi was there, his tail wagging nineteen to the dozen, his tongue waiting to lick Donald lovingly. The boy hugged him and tickled him and rolled him over. The corgi always loved that, for he had a great sense of fun.

Then into the next kennel, where the little poodle went nearly frantic with joy. She leapt straight into his arms, and covered his face with licks. She had missed him very much. Donald sighed happily. What a lot of love dogs had to give!

Then out he went, and into the next kennel belonging to the mongrel dog. He had gone nearly mad when he had heard Donald in the other kennels, talking to the alsatian, the corgi and the poodle. He threw himself at the boy, and began to bark for joy.

"Sh!" said Donald, in alarm. "You'll wake everybody, and I'll get into trouble. SHHH!"

The mongrel understood at once. He was a most intelligent dog, as mongrels so often are, and he certainly didn't want to get Donald into trouble. He calmed down, and contented himself with licking every single bare part of Donald he could find—knees, hands, face and neck!

"I do wish I'd thought of bringing a towel with me," said Donald, wiping his face with his hanky. "Now calm down—I'm going to see the labrador next door to you!"

But when he shone his torch into the next kennel, the labrador wasn't there. Another dog was there, a beautiful black, silky spaniel, the loveliest one that Donald had ever seen. He shone his torch on her, and she gave a little whine. She didn't know Donald. Who was this strange boy

She gave a small whine.

that all the other dogs seemed to welcome so lovingly?

"Oh—the labrador's gone back home, I suppose," said Donald, disappointed. "But what a

lovely little thing *you* are! And oh, what have you
got there—tiny puppies! Let me come in and
see them. I promise not to frighten them."

The spaniel listened to the boy's quiet voice
and liked it. She gave a small whine as if to say,
"Well, come in if you like. I'm proud of my little
family!"

So Donald opened the gate and went in. The
spaniel was a little wary at first, but Donald knew
enough of dogs to stand perfectly still for a minute
while she sniffed him all over, even standing up
on her hind legs to reach to his chest. Then she
gave a tiny bark that meant "Pass, friend. All's
well!" and licked his right hand with her smooth
tongue.

She went to her litter of tiny puppies and stood
by them, looking up as if to say, "Well? Aren't
they beautiful?"

"Yes, they are. And so are you," said Donald,
stroking the smooth, silky head of the proud
spaniel. "You must be the very, very valuable
spaniel that the vet told me was soon being sent
to him. He said you are worth a hundred guineas,
and that your puppies would be worth a lot of
money, too. Oh, I wish I'd been here when you
came, and could have looked after you, and
cleaned your kennel and given you water."

The spaniel curled herself round her litter of

puppies, and looked up happily at Donald. He gave her one last pat. "Goodnight. I'll leave you in peace with your little black pups."

He went out of the kennel and saw the alsatian

He laid his head on the dog's shoulder.

still standing with his paws on the top of his kennel-gate, listening for him. "I'll just come in again and keep you company for a little while," said the boy, and, to the dog's delight, he went into the kennel and sat down in the straw beside the big dog.

He laid his head on the dog's shoulder, and

Prince sat quite still, very happy. It was warm in
the kennel, and quiet. Don't go to sleep, Donald!
Your eyes are shutting. Wake up, Donald, someone's coming! WAKE UP!

DONALD was fast asleep. He was warm and comfortable and happy. The big alsatian kept very still, glad to feel the sleeping boy so near him, his ears pricked for the slightest sound. He felt as if he were guarding Donald.

Suddenly he began to growl. It was a very soft growl at first, for he did not want to disturb the boy. But soon the growl grew louder, and awoke Donald.

"What is it? What's the matter?" he asked Prince, who was now standing up, the hackles on his neck rising as he growled even more fiercely. Then he barked, and the sudden angry noise made Donald jump.

"What's up?" he said. "For goodness sake don't bring the vet out—he may not like my coming up here at night!"

But now the alsatian was barking without ceasing, standing up with his feet on the gate, wishing he could jump over it. A stranger was about, and the great dog was giving warning!

"I'd better go," thought Donald. "If the vet comes and finds me here, he may think it was I who disturbed the dogs. Gracious, they're ALL barking now! Can there possibly be anyone about? But why? No thief could steal one of these dogs—they would fly at him at once!"

The corgi was barking his head off, and so was the mongrel dog. Even the little poodle was yapping as loudly as she could. Only the black spaniel was quiet. Perhaps she was guarding her puppies, and didn't want to frighten them?

Donald climbed over the alsatian's gate, afraid that if he opened it, the great dog would rush out, and it might be very very difficult to get him back! He was amazed to see somebody coming out of the *spaniel's* kennel gate! There was very little moon that night, and all the boy could see was a dark figure, shutting the gate behind him.

"There's two of them!" said Donald to himself, as he saw someone else nearby. "What are they doing? Good gracious, surely they can't be stealing the spaniel's puppies? Where's my torch? I must go to her kennel at once!"

The two dark shadows had now disappeared silently into the bushes. Donald took his torch from his pocket and switched it on. He ran to the spaniel's kennel and shone the light into it.

"The spaniel's still there," he thought, "Lying quite still as if she's asleep. I'd better go in and see if all her puppies are beside her."

So in he went, and shone his torch on to the

sleeping dog. Alas, alas—not one single puppy was beside her! She lay there alone, head on paws, eyes shut.

"How can she sleep with all this row going on,

"What are you doing here?"

every single dog barking the place down!" thought Donald. "She must be ill!"

He touched the dog—she was warm, and he felt her breath on his hands. He shook her. "Wake up—someone has taken your puppies! Oh dear, those men must have knocked you out! They were afraid you'd bite them, I suppose! Wake up!"

But the spaniel slept on. Donald stood up and wondered what to do. The thieves had a good start now—he wouldn't be able to catch them. But wait—he knew Someone who *could* trail them —Someone who wouldn't stop until he had caught up with the wicked thieves!

He rushed back to the alsatian's kennel. The dog was still barking, as were all the others. "Prince, Prince, you're to go after those men!" shouted Donald, swinging open the great gate. "Get them, boy, get them! Run, then, RUN!"

The great alsatian shot off like an arrow from a bow, bounding along, barking fiercely. He disappeared into the darkness, the trail of the thieves fresh to his nose. Ah—wherever they had gone, wherever they hid, the alsation would find them!

Donald suddenly found his knees shaking, and he felt astonished. "I'm not frightened! I suppose it's all the excitement. Oh, those lovely puppies! I do hope we get them back!"

And then somebody came up at a run, and caught hold of him. "What are you doing here? Why have you roused the dogs! You deserve to be whipped!"

It was the vet! He couldn't see that the boy he had caught was Donald. He gave him a good shaking, and Donald fell to the ground when he had finished.

"Don't, sir, don't!" he cried, struggling up. "I'm Donald, not a thief. Sir, thieves have been here tonight and have stolen the spaniel's puppies, and . . ."

"What! Those wonderful pups!" shouted the vet, and rushed to the spaniel's kennel. He shone a powerful torch there. "I must get the police. I heard the dogs barking, and came as soon as I could. But what on earth are *you* doing here this time of night?"

"I couldn't sleep so I just came up to be with the dogs," said Donald. "I know it sounds silly, but it's true. I've missed them so. And I fell asleep in the alsatian's kennel, and only woke up when the thieves came. They got away before I could do anything."

The vet shone his torch in the direction of Prince's kennel. "The door's open!" he cried. "The dog's gone!"

"Yes. I let him out, to go after the thieves," said Donald. "You told me once that alsatians are often used as police dogs—for tracking people— and I thought he *might* catch the thieves."

"Donald—you're a marvel!" said the vet, and to the boy's surprise, he felt a friendly clap on his back. "Best thing you could have done! He'll track the thieves all right—*and* bring them back here. I wouldn't be those men for anything!

Now—we'll just ring up the police—and then make ourselves comfortable in Prince's kennel—and wait for him to come trotting up with those two wicked men! Ha—they're going to get a very —unpleasant—surprise!"

IT WAS very exciting, sitting in Prince's
kennel in the dark, waiting for the alsatian
to come back. The vet and Donald were not
the only two waiting there—two burly policemen
were there also!

The vet had telephoned to the police station
and the Sergeant and a policeman had cycled up
at once, as soon as they heard what had happened. "Good idea of that boy's, to send the dog
after them," said one man. "Very smart. Wish
I had a dog like that!"

The other dogs were awakeand restless, especially the spaniel, who missed her puppies, and
whined miserably. The men in the alsatian's
kennel talked quietly, and Donald listened, half-
wondering whether this could all be a dream.
Then suddenly the mongrel gave a small, quiet
bark.

"That's a warning bark," said the vet, in a low
tone. "Shouldn't be surprised if Prince has found
those men already, and is on his way back with
them."

Soon the other dogs barked too, and the two
policemen stood up, and went silently into the
dog-yard. The vet and Donald stood up too. The

The beam picked out two terrified me

boy felt his knees beginning to shake with excitement again. He heard a fierce growl not far off, and a sharp bark. Yes—that was Prince all right! And what was that groaning, stumbling noise?

"That's my dog coming," said the vet, "and by the sound of it, he's got the men. I can hear them stumbling through the wood. I only hope they've brought back the pups."

As the stumbling footsteps grew nearer, the police moved forward, and shone a powerful

d a great dog behind, his teeth bared.

torch into the nearby bushes. The beams picked
out two terrified men—and a great dog behind,
his teeth bared, and a continuous growl coming
from his throat—Prince, the alsatian! He had
followed the trail of the men for a mile—and
caught up with them! How frightened they must
have been when he rounded them up!

"Stand where you are!" said the Sergeant's
voice, sharply. "You're under arrest. Where are
the puppies?"

"Look here—that brute of a dog has bitten

me!" said one of the men, holding out a bleeding hand. "I want a doctor."

"You can wait," said the Sergeant. "A police van will be up here in a few minutes, and I'll take you down to the police-station, both of you. Where are the puppies?"

"We don't know," said the other man, sullenly. "We dropped them when we found this dog chasing us. Goodness knows where they are!"

"That dog's a dangerous one," said the other man, eyeing Prince carefully. "He nipped my friend too—on the leg."

"Serves you right," said the vet. "Look, Sergeant, I've *got* to find those pups, or they'll all die. They need their mother. Will you see to these men, and I'll go off with Prince and see if he can find the pups for me."

"May I come too?" asked Donald, eagerly.

"Yes. You may as well see this night's adventure to the very end!" said the vet, taking the boy's arm. "He's done well, hasn't he, Sergeant?"

"My word he has!" said the man. "Pity he's not in the police-force! Maybe you will be some day, young fellow."

"I shan't," said Donald. "I'm going to be a vet. I could train police-dogs for you then, if you like!"

That made everyone laugh. Then the vet gave the boy a little push. "Come on, old son—we've got to find those puppies within an hour or so, or we may lose one or two of them—they'll be scared, and very hungry. Prince! Go find, Prince! Find my spaniel puppies."

The black spaniel, still wide awake, was surprised at all the noise, and sad at the loss of her tiny puppies. She suddenly gave a sharp bark. "She says she wants to come too," said Donald.

"Right. We'll take her," said the vet, and the little company set off through the bushes—first Prince, the alsatian, then the vet with a basket, then Donald, then the spaniel, nosing behind.

"How will Prince know where those men threw down the puppies?" asked Donald, as they went through the woods, the vet's torch throwing a bright beam before them.

"Well, he must have passed near them, when he trailed those men," said the vet. "He'll remember all right. You can't beat an alsatian for tracking man or animal! Hi, Prince—don't go too fast. The spaniel can't keep up with us!"

Prince went steadily on his way, standing still at times to sniff the air. After he had gone about half a mile he stopped. The spaniel gave an excited bark and ran forward.

"Prince has smelt the pups," said the vet. "So has the spaniel. Don't go any further. Let her go forward to them first."

The spaniel forced her way through the under-growth, barking excitedly. Then she suddenly stopped and nosed something, whining in delight.

There lay the puppies, every one of them!

The vet shone his torch on her—and there, in the grass, lay the puppies, every one of them! The mother licked them lovingly, and then looked up at the vet. She turned back and tried to pick up one of the pups in her mouth. She must carry it home!

"It's all right, old lady," said the vet, in the same special "animal" voice that Donald so often used. "It's all right. I've brought a basket, look—with a warm rug inside. You shall watch me put all the pups into it, and when I carry the basket you can walk back home with your nose touching it. They'll be safe—and you will soon be back in your kennel with them."

And then off went a little procession through the dark woods. First, Prince, very pleased with himself. Then the vet with the basket of pups. Then the spaniel, her nose touching the basket all the time. And last of all a very happy, excited boy—Donald. *What* a night! And oh, WHAT a good thing it was that he hadn't been able to sleep—and had slipped up to the kennels! Yes, Donald—that was very lucky. But you do deserve a bit of luck, you know!

WHEN the vet, Donald, and the dogs, at last arrived back at the kennels, the telephone bell was ringing. The vet sighed.

"I hope it's not someone to say they want me to go and look at a sick cat, or a moping monkey!" he said. "It's still the middle of the night, and I'm tired. Aren't you, Donald?"

"I am a bit," said Donald. "But I don't mind. It's been—well, quite an adventurous night, hasn't it?"

The vet went to the phone. "Hallo? Yes. Who is it? Oh, Donald's father! Yes, actually, Donald *is* here. I'm sorry you were worried. Er—well, apparently he couldn't sleep, so he popped up to be with my dogs. Good thing he did, too. We've had an exciting night—been after thieves—and caught them too. Donald's been quite a hero. Well—the boy's tired out now. Shall I give him a bed for the night? Yes, yes—I'd be glad to have him. Right. Goodnight!"

"Gracious—was that Dad?" said Donald, alarmed. "Was he very angry because I'd come up here in the middle of the night?"

"No. No, I don't think so," said the vet. "He

seemed very relieved to know you were here, safe and sound. You get off to bed, old son. You can have the room next to mine. Don't bother about washing or anything—you're tired out. Just flop into bed."

Donald fell asleep almost at once. He was tired out, as the vet had said, but very happy. What a good thing he had come up to the kennels—and had spotted those thieves! What a good thing that Prince had found those lovely little spaniel puppies! What a good thing that . . . but just then he fell fast asleep, and slept so very soundly that he didn't even stir until the vet came to wake him the next morning.

"Oh goodness—shall I be late for school?" said Donald, looking in alarm at his watch.

"No. Calm down. It's Saturday!" said the vet. "Your mother's been on the phone this morning— she sounds very excited about something—I won't tell you what! She says will you please come back in time for breakfast."

"Oh dear—I hope I'm not going to get into any more trouble!" said Donald, jumping out of bed.

"No, I don't somehow think you'll find trouble waiting for you!" said the vet. "Buck up, though —and come back and help me today if you're allowed to."

Donald dressed at top speed and shot home on

his bicycle. Would his father be angry with him for slipping away in the middle of the night? Well —it had been worth it! It was a pity he hadn't been able to go and see if the spaniel puppies were all well and happy this morning, but maybe he could come back later on in the day.

He arrived home, put his bicycle away, and ran in through the kitchen door. Mrs. Mawkins, the cook, called out to him as he came in.

"Oh there you are, Master Donald. Fancy you being in the papers this morning!"

Donald had no idea what she meant—but he soon knew! As soon as he went into the sitting room, his mother ran to meet him and gave him a hug.

"Donald! Oh Donald, I didn't know I had such a brave son!"

"Well done, my boy!" said his father, and clapped him on the back. "Fancy you being in the papers!"

Donald was astonished. He stared at his father, puzzled. "What do you mean, Dad?"

"Well, look here!" said his father, and showed him the first page of his newspaper—and there, right in the middle, was a paragraph all about Donald!

"Boy sends alsatian dog after thieves, in middle of night. Helps police to find priceless spaniel

puppies." And then came the story of how
Donald had gone up to the kennels in the middle
of the night, heard the thieves, sent the alsatian
after them—and all the rest!

A paragraph all about Donald!

"I suppose the police told the paper all that
last night," said Donald, astonished. "Mother,
I couldn't sleep for thinking of those dogs, that's
why I went up to them in the middle of the night.
I know you and Dad said I wasn't to go and help
the vet—but I did so want to see the dogs again.
I just felt sort of lonely."

"Well, all's well that ends well," said his father, feeling really very pleased with Donald. "Your mother and I are proud of you. We've been talking things over, and we're both agreed that you *shall* go and help the vet again . . ."

"Oh Dad! THANK you!" cried Donald, his heart jumping for joy. "Now I'll be able to see those spaniel puppies again that the thief took. Oh, they're beautiful! Oh, I wish I was rich enough to buy one! Oh, and that little kitten too. I wish I was rich enough to pay the vet to keep it for me! I wish I could buy a . . ."

"Well now, that's enough, Donald," said his father. "It's no good getting big ideas, especially while your school work is poor."

"What about your homework for the weekend?" said his mother. "You mustn't forget that, in all the excitement! What have you to do? Sums? An essay? Geography or history?"

"I've forgotten," said Donald, feeling suddenly down-hearted. "Bother it! Where did I put my exercise book? The homework I've to do for the weekend is written there. I don't feel AT ALL like doing any!"

He fetched his exercise book and turned to the page where instructions for his weekend homework were written down. "Here it is—oh blow, an *essay* again! *"Write down what you would like*

to be when you grow up, and give the reasons why."
Donald stared at it in sudden delight. "Why—I
can do *that!* I want to be a vet, of course—and I
know ALL the reasons why. I can put dogs and
cats and horses and birds and everything into *this*
essay. I'll write it at once, this VERY minute!"

IT WAS really very surprising to see Donald settling down so very happily to do his homework. "We usually have such silly, dull things to write about," he said. "Now *this* is *sensible*. I've plenty to say! I only hope there are enough pages to say it in."

It was while Donald was finishing the longest essay in his life that there came a knock at the door. It was a man from another newspaper, wanting to ask questions about Donald and his exciting night.

"I'm sorry," said his father. "The boy has had enough excitement. We don't want him to talk to newspaper men, and get conceited about himself."

"Oh, I only want to ask him a few questions," said the man. "Such as, what does he plan to be when he's grown up? Maybe a policeman, perhaps, catching robbers and the like?"

Donald, writing his essay, heard all this. He ran to the door. "Why—that's EXACTLY what I'm writing for my weekend essay!" he said, surprised. "I'm going to be a vet, of course. I'm putting down all my reasons. I've just finished!"

"And what are your reasons?" asked the man, smiling at Donald.

"Now listen," said Donald's father, pushing the boy away. "We've told you that we don't want our son to think himself too clever for words, and to get conceited! The most we'll let you do is to read what he has written."

"Let me just have a look at it, then," said the man. Donald handed the exercise book to him and the man glanced quickly down the essay.

"Good, good, GOOD!" he said. "Best essay I've read for ages—straight from the heart—you mean every word of it, don't you, youngster? Do you get top marks every week for your essays? You ought to."

"No. I'm pretty well always bottom," said Donald. "But this is different. It's something I *like* writing about, something I *want* to write about. I know all about a vet's work, you see. It's *grand*."

"Go away now, Donald," said his father, anxious not to let the boy talk too much. "Leave your essay with me."

Donald went off, and his father turned to the waiting newspaper man. "You can have this essay of his, instead of talking to him, if you like. But I think you should pay the lad for it, you know, if you want to print it. I'll put the money into the bank for him."

"Right. Here's five pounds," said the man,

much to the astonishment of Donald's father. "And if that form master of his marks him bottom for *this* essay, well, all I can say is, the man doesn't know his job! I'll take it with me, have

"I'm going to be a vet, of course."

it copied, and send back the essay in time for him to take it to school next week. Thank you, sir. Good-day!"

And away went the man, looking very pleased with himself. "Ha!" he thought, "fancy that kid writing such an interesting piece about a vet's work, and all his animals—most remarkable! Good boy that. Deserves to have animals of his own. Funny there wasn't even a dog about the place—or a cat! Well, maybe the five pounds would help him to buy a pet for himself!"

Donald's mother and father were very proud and pleased to have been given five pounds for his essay. They went to tell Donald.

"Good *gracious*! Five pounds for a school essay!" said the boy, astounded. "I wish I'd written it better. It isn't worth ten pence, really. And I bet I'll be bottom in class as usual! But I *say—five pounds*! Now—what shall I spend it on?"

"Well—I shall put it in the bank for you, of course!" said his father. The boy stared at him in dismay.

"Oh *no* Dad! I want to *spend* it—spend it on something I badly want! It's *my* money. Mother, please ask Daddy to let me have it."

"Yes. Yes, I think you *should* have it, dear," said his mother, very proud of all that Donald had done the night before. "Give it to him, Dad—we'll let him spend it on whatever he likes. He shall choose!"

"Whatever I like, Mother—do you REALLY mean that?" cried Donald. "You won't say no to *anything*?"

"Well—you've been such a brave lad, quite a hero—and I think for once in a way you should do as you please," said his mother.

"Mother—if I buy a puppy with it, will you say no?" asked Donald.

"I'll say *yes*, you deserve one," said his mother, and his father nodded his head too.

"And—suppose I asked you if I could have a little hurt kitten that the vet's keeping for me—would you mind?" asked the boy. "It has only half a tail, because a dog bit it, so it's not beautiful —but I do love the little thing. That's really why I went to work for the vet—because he took the kitten and tended it, and kept it—and when he said he would send the bill in to Dad, I said no, I'd work for him, and he could keep my earnings to pay for the kitten."

His mother suddenly put her arms round him and gave him a warm hug.

"You can have a dog, a cat, a kitten, a monkey, anything you like! We didn't know quite what a clever son we had, nor how brave he is. We know better now. We're very very proud of you, Donald."

"Oh *Mother*! A dog of my own—a kitten! Oh, and I might get a donkey, if I save up enough. He could live in the vet's field. And I'll buy a cage and keep budgies—blue ones and green ones. Oh, I can't believe it!"

"And if Mr. Fairly, that form-master of yours, gives you low marks for that fine essay, I'll have something to say to him!" said Donald's father. "Well, well—I suppose we must now give up the idea of your being an architect when you grow up, Donald. It will be fun to have a vet in the family, for a change! I'm proud of you, son—I really am!"

D ONALD'S father kept his word. He
didn't put the five pounds into the bank
—he gave it to Donald. "Gracious—how
rich I am!" said the boy, delighted. "Mother,
do you mind if I go up to see the vet—and tell him
about the money?"

"Off you go!" said his mother. "But please
come back for dinner—I'm going to arrange a
very special one for you!"

Donald shot off to the vet's on his bicycle. He
whistled as he went, because he felt so happy. To
think that last night he was so unhappy that he
couldn't even go to sleep—and today he was too
happy for words! All because he rushed off to see
the dogs in the middle of the night!

The vet was delighted to see him again so soon
—and whistled in surprise when he saw the five
pound notes that the boy showed him. "Well,
well—writing must be a paying job, if you can
earn five pounds for an essay!" he said. "It takes
me quite a time to earn *that* amount!"

"Sir, would you please sell me one of those
beautiful spaniel puppies?" said Donald, earn-
estly. "I want one more than anything in the
world. A dog of my own—just imagine! Someone

who'll understand my every word, who'll always know what I'm feeling and will never let me down, because he will be my very faithful friend."

"Well, if ever a boy deserved a dog, it's you, Donald," said the vet. "But I'm not going to let you buy one of those pups, I'll *give* you one. I meant to, anyway, for what you did last night, and for all the help you've given me. You shall choose your own pup. Come along—let's see which one you want, before anyone else has their pick."

Donald was speechless. His face went bright red, and the vet laughed. "Can't you say a single word? And there's another thing—that little kitten is well enough to go now—I know you want her. You can have her too. Let her and the pup grow up together."

"Thank you, THANK YOU!" said Donald, finding his tongue. "But please, I've plenty of money now! I can pay for them both."

"I know. But if you really *are* going in for animals, you'll want kennels and cages and things," said the vet. "I'll show you how to *make* them— much cheaper than buying them—all you'll have to do is to buy the wood and the nails. You're good with your hands—you'll enjoy making things."

"It all seems rather like a dream," said Donald,

as they went to look at the puppies. "I was so miserable yesterday—and today I feel on top of the world! Oh I say, aren't the puppies *lovely*? They seem to have grown since last night. That little fellow is trying to crawl!"

The spaniel's mother looked up at them out of beautiful brown eyes. With her nose she gently pushed one of the puppies towards Donald. "That's the one she wants you to have!" said the vet. "It's the best of the lot."

And that is the one Donald chose. He left it with the mother till it was old enough to be his— and now he is making a fine kennel for it! "It will be yours when you are old enough," he tells the puppy. "I expect the kitten will sometimes sleep in your kennel with you, so I'll bring her along soon so that you can make friends."

He went to tell his Granny about the dog he had chosen. She listened, very pleased. "Well, well—I meant to give you a puppy myself, for your birthday, if your mother said yes—and now you have won one for yourself, by working for the vet. You deserve a dog, Donald, and I know you'll train him well. I can't give you a dog, now you have one—so I think I'll buy you a really good dog basket, so that you can have him in your room at night, to guard you when you're asleep!"

"That puppy is going to be very lucky!" said

Donald. "I'm making him a *lovely* kennel—the vet's helping me. We went and bought the wood together, out of the money I won for that essay. I've a kitten too—the one whose tail was half-bitten off by a dog. And I *think* I'm going to breed

"That's the one she wants you to have."

budgerigars, Granny. I've still enough money out of my five pounds to buy a breeding-cage. I'm going to give *you* my first baby budgie. Would you like a green or a blue one?"

"Oh—a green one, I think," said Granny. "It will match my curtains! Bless you, Donald—you do deserve your good luck. You earned it

yourself—and that's the best good luck there is!"
Donald still goes up to help the vet, of course,

"Would you like a green or a blue one?"

and you should have seen him one week when the
vet was ill! He looked after all the dogs, the cats,
the birds—and a little sick monkey! How happy

and proud he was! How good it felt to go round
and see every animal, big or small, look up in
delight when he came . . . yes, Donald—you'll
be a fine animal-doctor, when the time comes!

Prince, the alsatian, has gone back to his own
home now, of course—but Donald often sees him
when he goes out. Prince always sees him first,
though! Donald suddenly hears a soft galloping
noise behind him—and then he almost falls over
as the big alsatian flings himself on the boy,
whining and licking, pawing him lovingly.

"Do you still remember that exciting night in
the dark woods?" says Donald, ruffling the thick
fur round the dog's neck. "Remember those
little spaniel puppies? Do you see this beautiful
black spaniel at my heels—he was one of the
pups we rescued that night, you and I! I chose
him for myself. *Dear* old Prince. I'll never forget
you!"

One day you may meet a boy walking over
the grassy hills somewhere—a boy with five or
six dogs round him, dogs that come at his slightest
whistle. It will be Donald, taking out the kennel-
dogs for the vet, letting them race and leap and
play to their hearts' content. Call out to him—
"DONALD! Which is *your* dog?"

But you'll know which it is without his telling
you—that silky black spaniel beside him. What's

its name? Well, call "Bonny, Bonny, Bonny" and it will come rushing over to you at once!

Goodbye, Donald. Goodbye, Bonny. Good luck to you both. You deserve it!

Other great reads 🦊 *from* **Red Fox**

Further Red Fox titles that you might enjoy reading are listed on the following pages. They are available in bookshops or they can be ordered directly from us.

If you would like to order books, please send this form and the money due to:

ARROW BOOKS, BOOKSERVICE BY POST, PO BOX 29, DOUGLAS, ISLE OF MAN, BRITISH ISLES. Please enclose a cheque or postal order made out to Arrow Books Ltd for the amount due, plus 75p per book for postage and packing to a maximum of £7.50, both for orders within the UK. For customers outside the UK, please allow £1.00 per book.

NAME_____

ADDRESS_____

_____

Please print clearly.

Whilst every effort is made to keep prices low, it is sometimes necessary to increase cover prices at short notice. If you are ordering books by post, to save delay it is advisable to phone to confirm the correct price. The number to ring is THE SALES DEPARTMENT 071 (if outside London) 973 9700.

Other great reads from **Red Fox**

Adventure Stories from Enid Blyton

THE ADVENTUROUS FOUR

A trip in a Scottish fishing boat turns into the adventure of a lifetime for Mary and Jill, their brother Tom and their friend Andy, when they are wrecked off a deserted island and stumble across an amazing secret. A thrilling adventure for readers from eight to twelve.

ISBN 0 09 947700 9   £2.50

THE ADVENTUROUS FOUR AGAIN

'I don't expect we'll have any adventures *this* time,' says Tom, as he and sisters Mary and Jill arrive for another holiday. But Tom couldn't be more mistaken, for when the children sail along the coast to explore the Cliff of Birds with Andy the fisher boy, they discover much more than they bargained for . . .

ISBN 0 09 947710 6   £2.50

COME TO THE CIRCUS

When Fenella's Aunt Jane decides to get married and live in Canada, Fenella is rather upset. And when she finds out that she is to be packed off to live with her aunt and uncle at Mr Crack's circus, she is horrified. How will she ever feel at home there when she is so scared of animals?

ISBN 0 09 937590 7   £1.99

Other great reads from **Red Fox**

School stories from Enid Blyton

THE NAUGHTIEST GIRL IN THE SCHOOL

Elizabeth knows that she's going to hate boarding school and decides that the only way to get out of it is to be so naughty that she's sent straight home again. So she sets out to do just that – stirring up all sorts of trouble and getting herself the name of the bold bad schoolgirl. She's sure all she wants is to go home again, until she realises, to her surprise, that there are some things she hadn't reckoned with. Like making friends . . .

ISBN 0 09 945500 5   £2.99

THE NAUGHTIEST GIRL AGAIN

Elizabeth Allen is back at school for her second term and this time she's *not* going to be the naughtiest girl in the school any more . . . or so she thinks. It isn't as easy as all that though, and it seems that even when she's trying to be good, things still keep going wrong. So who is Elizabeth's secret enemy who wants her to get in trouble?

ISBN 0 09 915911 2   £2.99

THE NAUGHTIEST GIRL IS A MONITOR

Third term at Whyteleafe and to her surprise, Elizabeth is chosen to be a monitor. She tries her very best to set a good example to the other children but somehow things go wrong for her and soon she is in just as much trouble as she was in her first term, when she was the naughtiest girl in the school!

ISBN 0 09 945490 4   £2.99

Other great reads *from* **Red Fox**

Enid Blyton good value omnibus editions

MR TWIDDLE STORIES

Mr Twiddle is a silly but lovable old man. He's always losing things—like his hat and his specs—he has trouble with a cat, gets bitten by a goose and, no matter how he tries, he just can't remember anything! This collection contains two complete books in one!

ISBN 0 09 965560 8   £2.50

MR PINKWHISTLE STORIES

Mr Pinkwhistle is small and round with pointed ears and bright green eyes. And he can do all sorts of magic . . . This collection gives you two complete books about Mr Pinkwhistle in one!

ISBN 0 09 954200 5   £2.50

MR MEDDLE STORIES

Mr Meddle is a naughty little pixie who simply *can't* mind his own business. He always tries to help others but by the time he's fed birdseed to the goldfish, sat in the butter, gone to bed in the wrong house and chased a policeman, people usually wish they'd never set eyes on him. This collection of stories gives you two complete books about Mr Meddle in one!

ISBN 0 09 965550 0   £2.50

Other great reads ✎ *from* **Red Fox**

Animal stories from Enid Blyton

If you like reading stories about animals, you'll love Enid Blyton's animal books.

THE BIRTHDAY KITTEN

Terry and Tessie want a pet for their birthday – but when the big day comes, they're disappointed.

ISBN 0 09 924100 5   £1.99

THE BIRTHDAY KITTEN and
THE BOY WHO WANTED A DOG

A great value two-books-in-one containing two stories about children and their lovable pets.

ISBN 0 09 977930 7   £2.50

HEDGEROW TALES

Go on a journey through the woodlands and fields and meet the fascinating animals who live there.

ISBN 0 09 980880 3   £2.50

MORE HEDGEROW TALES

A second set of animal stories packed with accurate details.

ISBN 0 09 980880 3   £2.50

THE ADVENTURES OF SCAMP

Scamp the puppy is nothing but a bundle of mischief – and he does get into a lot of trouble.

ISBN 0 09 987860 7   £2.99

Other great reads from **Red Fox**

All the fun of the fair with Enid Blyton's circus stories

Roll up! Roll up! Discover Enid Blyton's exciting circus stories for yourself. They're full of adventure and thrills, with a colourful cast of funny and unusual characters and lovable animals. Join the children who live in the circus and enjoy all the fun of the fair for yourself.

MR GALLIANO'S CIRCUS

Jimmy loves the circus – how can he bear it to leave town? Is there *any* hope he might go with it?

ISBN 0 09 954170 X   £1.75

CIRCUS DAYS AGAIN

A new ringleader arrives at Mr Galliano's circus – and, oh dear! No one can *bear* him . . .

ISBN 0 09 954180 7   £1.75

COME TO THE CIRCUS

Fenella is terrified of animals. Imagine her horror when she discovers she is going to live in Mr Carl Crack's circus!

ISBN 0 09 937590 7   £1.75

THREE BOYS AND A CIRCUS

Orphan Dick is thrilled to find a job at the circus – but he has an enemy who wants him to leave.

ISBN 0 09 987870 4   £2.99

Other great reads from Red Fox

Discover the great animal stories of Colin Dann

JUST NUFFIN

The Summer holidays loomed ahead with nothing to look forward to except one dreary week in a caravan with only Mum and Dad for company. Roger was sure he'd be bored.

But then Dad finds Nuffin: an abandoned puppy who's more a bundle of skin and bones than a dog. Roger's holiday is transformed and he and Nuffin are inseparable. But Dad is adamant that Nuffin must find a new home. Is there *any* way Roger can persuade him to change his mind?

ISBN 0 09 966900 5   £2.99

KING OF THE VAGABONDS

'You're very young,' Sammy's mother said, 'so heed my advice. Don't go into Quartermile Field.'

His mother and sister are happily domesticated but Sammy, the tabby cat, feels different. They are content with their lot, never wondering what lies beyond their immediate surroundings. But Sammy is burningly curious and his life seems full of mysteries. Who is his father? Where has he gone? And what is the mystery of Quartermile Field?

ISBN 0 09 957190 0   £2.99

Other great reads ✦ from **Red Fox**

THE SNIFF STORIES   Ian Whybrow

Things just keep happening to Ben Moore. It's dead hard avoiding disaster when you've got to keep your street cred with your mates *and* cope with a family of oddballs at the same time. There's his appalling 2½ year old sister, his scatty parents who are into healthy eating and animal rights and, worse than all of these, there's Sniff! If only Ben could just get on with his scientific experiments and his attempt at a world beating *Swampbeast* score . . . but there's no chance of that while chaos is just around the corner.

ISBN 0 09 975040 6   £2.99

J.B. SUPERSLEUTH   Joan Davenport

James Bond is a small thirteen-year-old with spots and spectacles. But with a name like that, how can he help being a supersleuth?

It all started when James and 'Polly' (Paul) Perkins spotted a teacher's stolen car. After that, more and more mysteries needed solving. With the case of the Arabian prince, the Murdered Model, the Bonfire Night Murder and the Lost Umbrella, JB's reputation at Moorside Comprehensive soars.

But some of the cases aren't quite what they seem . . .

ISBN 0 09 971780 8   £2.99

Other great reads ✎ *from* **Red Fox**

Discover the wacky world of Spacedog and Roy by Natalie Standiford

---

Spacedog isn't really a dog at all – he's an alien lifeform from the planet Queekrg, who just happens to *look* like a dog. It's a handy form of disguise – but he's not sure he'll *ever* get used to the food!

SPACEDOG AND ROY

Roy is quite surprised to find an alien spacecraft in his garden – but that's nothing to the surprise he gets when Spacedog climbs out.

ISBN 0 09 983650 5   £2.99

SPACEDOG AND THE PET SHOW

Life becomes unbearable for Spacedog when he's entered for the local pet show and a French poodle falls in love with him.

ISBN 0 09 983660 2   £2.99

SPACEDOG IN TROUBLE

When Spacedog is mistaken for a stray and locked up in the animal santuary, he knows he's in big trouble.

ISBN 0 09 983670 X   £2.99

SPACEDOG THE HERO

When Roy's father goes away he makes Spacedog the family watchdog – but Spacedog is scared of the dark. What can he do?

ISBN 0 09 983680 7   £2.99

Join the RED FOX Reader's Club

The Red Fox Readers' Club is for readers of all ages. All you have to do is ask your local bookseller or librarian for a Red Fox Reader's Club card. As an official Red Fox Reader you will qualify for your own Red Fox Reader's Clubpack – full of exciting surprises! If you have any difficulty obtaining a Red Fox Readers' Club card please write to: Random House Children's Books Marketing Department, 20 Vauxhall Bridge Road, London SW1V 2SA.

THE ENID BLYTON NEWSLETTER

Would you like to receive The Enid Blyton Newsletter? It has lots of news about Enid Blyton books, videos, plays, etc. There are also puzzles and a page for your letters. It is published three times a year and is free for children who live in the United Kingdom and Ireland.

If you would like to receive it for a year, please write to: The Enid Blyton Newsletter, PO Box No. 357, London WC2E 9HQ, sending your name and address. (UK and Ireland only).